The B

Matchmaking Club Book 1

By

Joanna Mazurkiewicz

Chapter One

"I'm a matchmaker, Aubrey," I rolled my eyes, "not cupid." But I wasn't sure the message was getting through to her. Aubrey twirled her deep red hair, seeming unconvinced, sliding me another shot across the bar. I raised a brow, sighed, said nothing more and downed it quickly as I scanned the bar from the corner of my eye. The dim blue lighting wasn't making it any easier, and the song was horribly distracting as the beat vibrated from the floor to my chest. "This could've been done better in the daylight."

"Lily, please." She sighed. "Just…size him up for me?"

"Do you not understand how we work?" I scoffed. "If I haven't attended one social with this guy or even talked to him—"

"Take all the time you need!" she pleaded. "I just want you to get a first impression before anything else happens. I've heard you…you *catch vibes*?"

"Why do I feel like you talked to—"

"Alex Sherman?"

"Yeah, the Chad with the good weed, right?"

She nodded quickly.

"I don't 'catch vibes,' Aubrey." I threw up my fingers in quotation marks. "I notice patterns. My first word is often my final. I hope you know that."

Taking in my surroundings of the bar again, I narrowed my eyes in on two men who had just slid into a booth across the room, and an alarm went off in my head. A hand clutched my forearm, and I knew I was looking at the right guy.

"Aubrey…" I almost groaned. "You can't go after him."

"Why not?" she whined, and I regretted taking her up on her special request.

"See here, *this* is why I ask for names." I lightly pounded my fist against the table, giving her a stern look. "The world of billionaires can't guarantee you anonymity. Especially not with me. Why do you think detectives approach me first when it comes to domestic violence issues?"

"Could you cut it out and just tell me?" she snapped.

"The guy's *married.*" I slid the glass toward her, watching as it clinked against her *own* engagement ring. "In fact, I was the one who set him up in the first place!"

"With *who?*" she squeaked, but I shook my head. Aubrey was desperate, and I needed to make sure there was enough distance between her and her prey. *Again!*

Matchmaking wasn't exactly being cupid, but I did ensure that my services gave someone value for their money. That meant keeping the couples I paired together for as long as possible. Aubrey Holland's helpless romanticism wasn't a secret in the industry. I wondered how many matchmakers she'd gone through before coming to me as a last resort. This was the sixth guy Aubrey had asked me to check out for her this year alone, and that wasn't a good look for me. But while being engaged? That was a little new.

"What happened to Fernando?" I wagged my pen at her. She slid yet another shot glass toward me, but I pushed it back.

She'd definitely fucked up with him, hadn't she?

Aubrey looked away, obviously holding back tears that were threatening to spill. With a large gulp of my rejected shot, she dabbed a tissue under her eyes, and I groaned internally, hoping I wasn't in for another episode of her dramatics.

Why do I continue to put up with this? I sighed to myself before realizing she paid well, and consistently, too.

"I know he proposed and all but"—She sniffled lightly—"I think he might be cheating on me."

Coughing a little, I waved the bartender over for some water. She quickly complied, and I downed it just as fast.

"Well, I did warn you."

"But I really liked him." Her voice was trembling.

"You're still wearing the ring."

She took it off and threw it on the countertop. I watched the amethyst and diamond-studded ring bounce off the marble, glint in the light, and drop onto the floor beside the bartender, who looked very sorry for Aubrey as she burst into sobs. And I wished I could feel as bad, had this not happened for the third time now.

But I wasn't her therapist, nor was I her friend.

I was a matchmaker, and there were no matches here.

Kicking the door closed, I heaved myself onto the couch face-first. My heels fell off onto the carpet with a light thud, and I heard Holly's snuffles around my feet. She must've been hungry, considering how long I had been out.

"I'm sorry, sweetie." I petted the collie who was giving me her largest puppy-dog eyes that prompted me onto my tired feet immediately. Holly needed food, and so did I.

"Alexa, play some music."

The apartment was flooded in light upbeat music, but each day I walked in here it just…felt emptier than before. When I had felt this way five years ago, I'd thought it was because I'd just moved in and I needed to own the space. In an attempt to make it my own, I marked the walls with memories and topped the shelves with my identity. This was the first time I'd ever had something that was mine. It was a home, something that I'd believed was impossible to attain.

So, now that I finally had everything I wanted, why did I still feel so empty?

Holly barked at me, snapping me out of my reverie. I blinked into the open fridge, wondering how I'd gotten here. I'd lived a lot of my life on autopilot, as part of trying to survive. It wasn't like that anymore, though, so why couldn't I just be normal?

Sighing, I sifted through the items inside before realizing that I didn't feel like cooking at all. I plucked my phone out of my pocket and surfed through Uber Eats, settling for Chinese takeout before going through my messages.

Seeing Mom had messaged, I groaned and opened it, playing her voice note as I reached for the box of dog food.

"*I know you're busy with work right now, sweetie, but will you be free tomorrow night to drop by? I met this adorable family on the cruise you sent me on, and they've taken me up on my offer for dinner.*"

"She's back already?" I whined to Holly and filled her bowl, who only munched on her Kibble in response. I got up, determined to draw myself a nice bath. God knew it would be the last time this month I'd have the chance to relax for longer than an hour.

"*They have a flight the next day so please don't miss out on this. They have a son and he's a surgeon! Very good looking, too.*"

I groaned at her giggle, knowing she would've shoved my pictures in his face and begged for him to get to know me.

"*Anyway, call me back! I haven't heard from you in so long. Love you!*"

Sure you do, I thought bitterly. Sometimes I wished I had the heart to treat her the same way she treated me before I hit the jackpot and opened my own business. It was hard work to run it, and today was only a reminder that it would get tougher.

Aubrey had taken a lot out of me. Against my better judgment like always, I'd stayed by her side and helped her work through her insecurities. As much as I tried to convince her that a break away from men would be a great idea, she wasn't having it. I wasn't exactly a therapist so I couldn't pry out the reason for her dependency on men, but good lord, she had terrible luck with them. Also, terrible taste. I just wished she'd let me pick out someone for her instead of insisting on my help for setting her up with whomever she liked on a whim.

Did I know Fernando was a cheater? Yes. And I did religiously remind her of his past. It was just hard to leave Aubrey alone in this, because deep down, I empathized with her a lot. As ditzy and airheaded as she was, she was one of the few people that searched for genuine love and connection. I had to admire her energy to keep at it after all the heartbreak she'd been through. Bless her heart.

Eight years in this industry revealed that four out of five men had cheated on their partners, no matter what stage of the relationship it was in. When men had money, the sex would come rolling in. When they felt the time was right or the girl was worth it, they'd settle. There was no point in pushing such people into a commitment before then. Although many married men weren't any better at keeping their vows, either.

The sad part about my job wasn't making sure these men wouldn't cheat, or that the couple would stay in love. It was all about keeping the money in the same place: within the elite. Calculating the couples' values, interests, and psychological patterns to ensure what circumstances in their nature would allow them to thrive financially. Cheating wasn't really an issue in most billionaire couples anymore. They had their sex parties, they had their younger boyfriends and girlfriends that they liked to spoil, and with a little communication between the parties, my couples' counsellor could convince them that it was just an honest, open relationship where everyone was happy without losing anything. Especially the money and their image. *And think of the kids. Oh, the kids…*

Money was just…so much more powerful than love, and I couldn't blame anyone for it. I didn't believe in love, I believed in power. And money was power. It was mine. It had gotten me out of a life that had almost collapsed in on itself.

If it wasn't money…the next powerful thing was death.

I was alone and I had money. And Holly. What more could I want?

Chapter 2

The party was in full swing by the time Aubrey and I arrived. The marble floor was glistening, chandeliers glittering with an array of precious stones (a beautifully commissioned piece) that cascaded the sunlight into rainbows against the walls. The wine was already flowing, although no one was drunk yet. There was light laughter and chatter in the air from people in soft, flowy dresses and light suits. It all reminded me of a more casual and modern version of the *Great Gatsby* party—in pastel. I looked down at my mint-green chiffon dress, and bronze skin peeking from beneath the slit up my thigh. I'd made a good choice with this dress, especially in pairing it with gold minimalist heels and jewelry.

Aubrey gripped my arm tight, almost cutting off my circulation and pointed to the pool in the center of the large room where flowers and candles floated peacefully.

"Don't worry." I patted her hand. "There's a plexiglass overlay on it."

Aubrey's acrylic nails pulled out of my skin, and I almost groaned from pain. One of Aubrey's exes had gotten a little too drunk for her liking at a New Year's Party and thought it would be a fun idea to push her into a pool as a prank. I'd warned her that the guy was notorious for humiliating anyone he was associated with, which was why so many people kept their distance. As charming as he seemed, he wasn't socially adept enough to hold himself accountable or responsible for anything.

"Do rich people always need a pool at their parties?" she grumbled.

"I don't know, Aubrey." I chuckled. "You tell me."

"My dad never had parties around pools," she huffed.

"How old are you again?"

"Twenty-five. Why?"

The tinkle of delicate glass echoed throughout the room, drawing everyone's attention to the center of the pool where a woman stood in a delicately embroidered cream-colored dress. Her honey-blonde hair was wrapped in a chignon much like mine, except it was neatly pulled away from her face, while some of my dark-brown strands framed my own.

"All right, remember what we came for." I tugged Aubrey's hand. She didn't need a reminder. Her eyes were already scanning the crowd like a lioness hunting for prey. Aubrey had let her red hair fall straight in a bob around her neck, wrapped in soft pink tulle and a simple silver necklace. She didn't hide her freckles, and her warm brown eyes were alight with excitement and nervousness.

"There he is," she gasped and nodded toward the large window where a tall blond man stood in a gray pinstriped suit, flanked by a man and a woman who appeared eerily similar with pale skin, black hair, and blue eyes. The blond guy had eyes equally as bright and blue as the other two, but looked considerably younger. They had to be siblings.

"Wait, which one are you going for?"

"The *blond* one. His name is Jacque Dupont."

It came as no surprise that I didn't recognize them, as I'd gone through the invitation list and noticed that there were around ten people here I hadn't heard of. Some were definitely foreigners from other countries here on business, but I hadn't realized so many of them were so…young.

I guessed the parents had brought their kids along to socialize and become familiar with such gatherings. What was I saying? I'd only just turned thirty myself. I was certain the youngest here was Aubrey.

"Does Mr. Holland know you've invited me as your plus one?" I asked. "Don't want the poor guy apologizing again for the next ten minutes when I see him."

"Do you think I give him anxiety?"

I lifted a brow. "*You* have anxiety."

"Fair. Now find out what you can."

I nodded and made my way around to him, making sure to stay out of their line of sight. I needed to appear beside him out of thin air, as if

I were just a forgettable bystander making small talk. Honestly, people like us could make great spies if given the opportunity. Minus life-threatening situations, of course.

Aubrey had seen him on Instagram, following a hashtag about this party to celebrate a new charity establishment as a result of the contributions of everyone in this very room. A state-of-the-art orphanage that ensured a bright future for all that found themselves there, with plans to extend the program further out and make it global. And, honestly, I didn't want to be suspicious about something so generous, but the rich didn't do anything without an ulterior motive or massive benefit to them.

This was Selene Alexakis and John Caron we were talking about, though—things could be different. Selene had a classic rags-to-riches tale where a rich man had fallen in love with her: a schoolteacher in an orphanage that had also worked night shifts as a bartender to make ends meet. But she was also cunning. As beautiful as Selene was, she knew she was just another exotic sidepiece for him to brag about on his yacht trips with his buddies. It hadn't been the first time she had been taken home by a rich man for a night, but she'd learned enough to understand how to get through to one. All it took was a conversation.

No one knew of the words spoken between them that night, but he was smitten with her to the point of eloping, and only returning once his child was born. His parents had been furious at his rebellion, as their family matchmaker had plans to betroth him into the Chevrolet family.

Honestly, Selene had just gotten extremely lucky with John Caron because he was kind of a sweet guy: meek, not very confrontational, and also a pushover. It had been why his decision to elope was such a shock because he was normally completely under his parents' thumb in all matters of his life.

I'd heard all this two years ago from the family matchmaker, Mrs. Beaumont, who was my former mentor. She'd admitted to being especially bitter at first, until she realized years later this was one of those rare instances that true love blossomed in the lives of the rich. Sure, Selene wasn't from the wealthiest of backgrounds, but she'd managed to capture the heart of someone like John and inspired him to stand up for what he wanted. And *that* was magical.

Of course, I'd just scoffed and laughed at the time. She'd laughed, too.

"As many disappointments as we see in our line of work, just remember, *mon papillon*"— Mrs. Beaumont leaned in—"a heart cannot be swayed."

Looking at John Caron moving toward his wife with a twinkle in his eye and love in his hands as they reached for her, I guessed she was right. For some lucky few, true love did exist. Selene was likely the kindest person to exist in the billionaire circles, so I hoped her plans would work the way she wanted them to.

That wasn't going to be me, though, so I needed to move and get to the siblings before I missed my opening for small talk because I was being paid good money for this. I could only hope that maybe someone existed for Aubrey, and she would find love just like Selene and John.

I walked casually behind the refreshments table, making a beeline for the pillar and standing behind it to assess my surroundings. Most people were still fixated on the couple, some breaking away every now and then for a slice of dessert or a drink. The blue-eyed siblings were still by the window, with the blonde sitting on the sill, appearing bored and chewing gum.

Keeping behind the pillars, I finally neared the window they were positioned around. The dark-haired boy had resorted to using his phone to kill time while the girl seemed like she was searching for someone. She soon walked away after spotting another girl in the crowd, who turned around and hugged her, erupting in excited whispers.

Narrowing my eyes at the boy, I prayed to whatever entities that existed he wasn't wearing air pods. Every time I was at a social and needed to assess the coming generation to profile them as suitors, I'd have to deal with that cursed invention. I once had to bump into a girl "accidentally" for her to take them off so we could talk. The young man was still too far away for me to get a good look at, so I dug into my purse for my tiny golden binoculars. *I know, silly, but some things need to happen from a distance before making the first move.*

No earbuds! I cheered internally and stuffed my binoculars away. Keeping to the wall and the spaces between people, I finally positioned myself about five feet away from my target. Noticing a server coming our way, I casually moved forward to pick up a drink off the tray and took a sip. I'd ended up just by the two men.

A round of applause filled the room, and the boys looked up to see what was going on. Observing from the corner of my eye, I found the blond man's eyes fall on Selene and John.

"She's beautiful, no?" I said, feigning distraction.

"She doesn't age…" He trailed off absently, and I glanced over to see his narrowed eyes fixated on her. "That's kind of suspicious. Do Greeks have vampires in their mythology?"

What even… I pondered in confusion, *Good grief he's probably an airhead…like Aubrey!*

"W-what? No, I'm not aware of any."

"But I know of Dracula's existence."

"That's Romanian history," I muttered with a sip to calm myself because I could feel the judgment coming on.

"Rome, Greece, same thing."

I choked on my rose vodka.

Definitely an airhead. How on earth did this guy get into the University of Paris?

"I'm guessing your parents also contributed to the orphanage program to be here."

"Kind of. They're mainly here to fix ties with Uncle John and his wife."

The surprise of it caught me off guard and I held onto the wall casually, trying to play it off. Mrs. Beaumont never mentioned this part of the story.

"Will it be awkward for you?"

"I don't know yet," he said thoughtfully. "We'll see at the dinner party."

"You'll be pretty bored until then," I suggested while tapping away on my phone and shooting Aubrey a message to bring herself over. This was so unconventional of me because it wasn't what matchmakers should be doing at all, but I figured Aubrey's anxiety had rendered her unable to communicate with strangers without assistance. Anyway, this was more like freelance than anything too serious. I was just doing what Aubrey wanted and being paid for it.

"Yeah." He sighed. "I don't know many people here."

"Would you like a tour of this place? It has incredible architecture." I asked quickly and waved Aubrey over discreetly to stand next to me. "My friend Aubrey Holland has been here quite often. Her parents are best friends with John and Selene. She could show you around."

I was hoping he would accept considering he was supposed to be studying architecture. I could see his eyes widen in curiosity and finally look over at us. He studied Aubrey's face curiously, who appeared a bit flushed beside me. I pinched her hand and she shot it forward to him.

"Hello." She greeted nervously. "You must be new here, huh?"

Jacque stood up and shook her hand softly, lips in a gentle smile as if trying to ease her.

"Yeah, I am. I've been wanting to take a look, but I didn't know if it would be inappropriate to leave the room to snoop around."

Jacque's entire demeanor had changed in an instant. What was with pretty girls having this effect on men? Like a gentleman, he lifted her hand and led her away. I watched the two, slightly impressed. That went a lot better than I expected. I smiled at their retreating backs and turned around, taking a sip of my drink, deciding to enjoy the party and socializing with the others here that I hadn't met before.

"*Oof!*"

People gasped nearby as I slipped from the impact against a literal wall and fell backward. I braced myself for the impact my poor butt would suffer but it never came. A strong grip around my bicep held me, suspended inches from the floor, and my nails dug desperately into the forearm of…

"Cristo?" I observed him carefully in confusion. How had he changed *that* much?

He wasn't just tanned, he was a brushed deep golden color. His gray eyes were stormy and so intense, with stubble that highlighted his sharp jaw and lifted his bone structure like a Greek god. I mean, he was half-Greek so I could see it. He'd taken good care of his hair: dark and slicked back over his head, swept a little to the side. I was absolutely stunned. He'd aged better than anyone else I knew. I didn't think anyone could be this good looking.

"Ah, you *remember* me." He chuckled with a wag of his finger. "Oops."

His grip disappeared and I finally found the floor, luckily it didn't hurt as bad as it would have had he not caught me previously.

"I see you remember me, too." I huffed as I pushed myself to stand. I felt a delicate hand at my bicep help me up. "Felicé, you gem, thank you. How's Howard?"

"He's doing all right." She kissed my cheek in greeting. "Hope the fall didn't hurt you too badly."

"I'll be all right." I smiled and she walked away, waving to Cristo in acknowledgment.

"Did you have to do that?" I snapped and dusted myself off, reaching for the handkerchief in his breast pocket to wipe away the alcohol stain on the skirt of my dress. I avoided looking him in the eyes and kept my head down. He was so tall, around six foot one, I guessed. I would have to crane my neck to look him in the eyes and doing that for too long would be painful.

"Consider it payback. You have a strong arm, though," he commented playfully. "I bet you punch harder, too."

"That was *one* time." I rolled my eyes.

Cristo Caron was the one and only son to Selene and John, and heir to Alexakis Enterprise. We'd only met once six years ago when I was tasked to profile him for an engagement request. We'd met at a quiet restaurant where he tried escaping from me by excusing himself to the bathroom. I'd waited for him at the back entrance of the kitchen with my arms crossed, unamused. I would've let him go if it hadn't been for Mrs. Beaumont's assignment. Part of the job was to learn to work with unwilling parties. They were usually the children of rich people.

I hadn't been sure how he managed to get past me and escape, but he was so fast. I still wasn't going to give up and followed him out, finding myself in a maze of dark alleyways. Ten minutes into the search, I'd run into a group of burly thugs and found myself cornered by them. Despite my fighting instincts kicking in, I knew I would die that day. It hadn't been the first time I'd been beaten up by men, but there was only so much I would be able to bear. Plus, those guys had weapons.

The next second, I was roughly pulled around the corner by someone. In my defense, it was a natural reflex to punch whoever it was.

"Ow…" Cristo breathed. "That was a good punch, lady."

"Cristo!"

"Leave this to me." He shook his head and took his jacket off to wrap around me. "I didn't mean for this to happen. I'm sorry."

The rest was history. I'd called the police, he'd ended up with a few bruises, but the other guys hadn't looked any better. Selene and John apologized to me profusely after collecting their son from the station and dropping me home. Of course, I told Mrs. Beaumont everything. The only thing she'd been concerned about was where Cristo had gotten his speed and cunning from.

I'd still failed that assignment, though.

"What brings you back to New York?" I held his handkerchief out to him. "I thought you wanted nothing to do with your parents after what happened that night."

"Haven't you heard? I'm in charge of designing the orphanages."

"Huh." I raised a brow. Why were so many rich kids interested in architecture these days? "Weren't you becoming a sculptor?"

"Double major." He grinned.

I couldn't understand how he had such a playful demeanor at thirty. I knew rich men were either pretty cocky or sophisticated, but playful? He had this gleam in his eyes that held a childlike innocence that even teenagers didn't have anymore. A server came over to hand him a suspiciously dark drink, who then fist-bumped him and went off.

I cocked a brow at him.

"Don't worry." He chuckled. "It's just a berry mix. I'm allergic to alcohol, remember?"

"Oh." I felt my face grow hot. I couldn't believe I'd forgotten. The reason I was so sought out was because I had an exceptionally good memory and remembered even the most insignificant details.

"What's wrong, Lilith?" He cocked his head with a smirk. "Getting a little old for this job?"

I balled up my fist, giving him a pointed expression, irritation crawling up my chest. Although what he said was perfectly harmless, I was hearing a lot of it from my mom, too. Getting too old for marriage, too old for children, too old for men. That I would be alone all of my life if I didn't find someone soon. It was the reason why I'd sent her on that cruise—to finally get some peace from the constant reminder that time was slipping by—and I still wasn't happy like I should be.

"You're too old to be fighting like this with Mark's mother, too," Her voice echoed through my head, *"It's been years, you know? Just let it go."*

The anger I was feeling was real, and I knew I was going to have to deal with yet another episode of PTSD on my own. I was angry at myself, too. How could something so small set me off so easily? I just wanted to have fun today.

I wanted to return with a snarky retort, but my mind had come up blank. All I could think of were vile responses that would be a little too personal for either of us. I wasn't the type to do that, and I understood alcohol was a touchy subject for him because he'd almost died a few times due to his allergy.

So, I simply turned away from him and walked off, deciding to go home. I wasn't in the right headspace to deal with him. I could feel his confused gaze burn into the back of my head.

"Lilith?"

I ignored him and kept walking.

I pushed open my apartment door, fell face-first onto the couch and let the heels fall off my feet. I cried. Holly sniffed around my feet and came to my face, with a curious yelp of alarm as she heard my sobs. I needed to be alone. It wasn't even 3 p.m. yet, and I was already an exhausted mess.

Holly licked my hand, and I lifted my head and looked at her through tears.

"Do you think they're right, Holly?" I sniffled. "Am I getting too old?"

She only barked in response and licked my cheek to wipe away the tears.

"I don't know what to do anymore." I hiccupped, pushing myself up to sit and patting my lap. Holly jumped on and snuggled her face into my neck. I held onto her and cried, still feeling lonely. Maybe lonelier than ever before.

I knew I needed therapy, but it was so hard to open up to people at all. I guessed I wasn't ready to try it yet. Medication? I was deathly scared of becoming dependent on pills, no matter how helpful they were. Trust issues were a given with everything I'd dealt with to make it here. But there was this glass wall between me and other people that I couldn't seem to break. I couldn't understand what was so different about me that caused me to feel this way. I had a fairly open-mind and could understand where someone was coming from. I could empathize with people easily and could hold a decent conversation with almost anyone.

Then why did I feel so alone? How did I know so many people but had no one to call a friend yet?

And what the hell was I going to wear to dinner at Mom's tonight?

Chapter 3

My fingers would break off if I wrung them anymore, but I couldn't help it. I'd made the right choice to wear a simple satin dress because I was sweating from all the nerves in the cool breeze under my black shawl. It was navy blue and fell just below my knees, which went well with the golden hoops. I wore the heels from earlier and had made sure to bring Holly with me. Mom's poodle, Cotton, got along well with her. She barked impatiently and I finally rung the bell.

I hadn't seen her in weeks, and it had been so peaceful without her. Seeing her tonight would mean opening the door I'd fought to lock on her. I left the mail slot open for her, but that was as far as I was willing to allow any communication to come through.

A full minute passed, and she hadn't answered. Hoping with all my heart that she'd forgotten about me, I turned around to leave. I could tell her I rang but she never answered, and my phone was dead so I couldn't even call. It would be a good enough excuse, and if she yelled, I'd hang up on her. Easy-peasy. She couldn't control me anymore, and she wouldn't have the energy to drive an hour and a half to my place to face me.

Knowing her, she would convince me to spend the night. I deliberately hadn't packed a bag, so there was no way she could make me even if she did open the do—

"Lilian!"

"It's Lilith, Mom…" I grunted and turned to face her. The distaste on my face must've been evident because her smile immediately slipped, and the familiar narcissistic scowl of disapproval crossed her countenance for a second.

"I gave you your name." She seethed, her voice dropping an entire octave. "Do not defy me."

"Maria, is she here?" another woman called excitedly from behind her. Mom's facial features lifted immediately, and she looked like a whole new person.

"Yes, this is Lilian." She grabbed my arm and pulled me inside. I stumbled on my heels but pulled myself together. As unfair as it was, I always felt so small around her even after all these years of being independent.

"Hi." I held my hand out to the petite blonde woman before me. She took it and gave it a gentle shake, which surprised me. She had an air about her that was calming. Her eyes were kind and bright, and she appeared older than my mom, but she seemed so much younger in her voice and demeanor.

"You really are as lovely as your mother described," she commented. "We thought you would be late, and we've just finished setting the table."

" It was a long drive," I said apologetically. "Please, let's eat. I'm starving."

We soon found ourselves at the dinner table where her husband greeted me: a tall man that smiled constantly and had a balding head. The woman's son was nowhere to be seen yet. I glanced at mom. She looked younger since the last time I saw her. Must've been the spa treatments I had started booking her into every week. She'd tinted her hair, and her hazel eyes were bright. I'd inherited them, sadly. Her voice was light and cheery, nothing like the voice I'd grown up with. She was being so nice, and I felt so…confused. She did this every time we had company. It wasn't new but caught me off guard every time. It always shocked me how easily she switched faces.

"Maria and I didn't get to talk much since we only met on the last day of the cruise, and we had to finish packing and disembark," the woman explained.

I still hadn't caught her name. Had Mom told me? I couldn't remember, which was funny considering how strong my memory usually was. I listened to her cheerful voice rather absently.

"Mom makes friends very easily." I chuckled through my teeth. I wasn't lying, Mom had such a charismatic façade that most people couldn't look past to see her true personality.

"So, tell us about yourself."

"She's a matchmaker." Mom interjected before I could say anything. "She works for billionaires and is paid *very well*."

"Mom." I sighed, pushing down the scathing hiss crawling up my throat.

"She's the best one in New York, Barbara," she continued, and I poured myself a glass of cold water to cool me down and keep my mouth occupied. I knew I would snap otherwise. "People come running to her when they finally stop whoring around." She laughed.

I stared at her absolutely horrified. I knew my grandparents were very conservative but that wasn't something she should just say out loud. The guests laughed politely but I could see they were uncomfortable.

"Ah, Marcus, we've been waiting for you," Mom said as a man walked into the dining room and I flinched, almost jumped out of my seat in fear actually. I soon realized she had said Marcus and not Mark, and I coughed uncomfortably. Everyone stared at me in concern, while Mom gave me a scornful glare.

"Holly brushed against my leg…I think." I chuckled. "I didn't know she was there."

Right on cue, as if the world were out to embarrass me, Holly and Poodle started barking at each other in the living room.

"Hey, you're Lilian, right?" The man swooped into the rescue, and I looked at him gratefully as he sat next to me. My mouth automatically opened to correct him, but I remembered Mom was still there, and I would need to try and keep the peace as best as I could at the table.

"Yes." I smiled as naturally as I could. His eyes smiled back at me. Marcus was a good-looking guy, fair skinned with wavy brown hair, smartly dressed, and maybe three inches taller than I was.

"We can start dinner now," Mom announced. "Please, help yourselves!"

Marcus and I made polite talk while Mom talked to his parents. It was as easy as slipping on a dress and imagining I was a character like Audrey Hepburn.

"Mom said you were a surgeon." I set my drink on the table.

"Cosmetic surgeon. Also, a dermatologist," he replied coolly. My face almost fell, and I knew exactly what was going on.

"Maybe you could fix her nose, Marcus," Mom joked. "Hers is quite crooked, isn't it?"

Marcus appeared stunned and his mouth fell open a bit. "Only barely, ma'am. It suits her. She's a beautiful woman."

My mouth fell open at the sheer courage he had to contradict her without a beat. My chest felt…warm.

"I was just joking." Mom chuckled with a hand over her mouth, but I knew she felt embarrassed. "It's sweet that you find her pretty."

Oh, great, now I would go home and stare at that small bump all day. My nose seemed straight from afar, but if someone looked too closely, then they'd notice it just slightly hooked. It felt so prominent when I was a child, and I'd always wanted a nose job. The moment I moved out, I realized it wasn't as prominent as I'd been made to believe.

I had enough issues to deal with, and I didn't need Mom bringing my old insecurities back. I knew coming here had been a terrible idea. If Mom made one more inappropriate comment, I knew I would cry.

"You look upset." He leaned in and whispered.

"I'd just forgotten what she was like." I chuckled lightly. "It's been over a month or so since I was last here. I usually only come to do a routine check-in and head back quickly."

"I can see that she could be a little… unpredictable."

"Funnily enough, I still haven't figured out how to navigate her moods."

He took a sip of his drink. "If it's any comfort, she had more good than bad to say about you."

"I'm aware of her routine." I smiled. "She doesn't want to scare off possible suitors."

He laughed. "So that's what this is about, huh?"

"I'm just as mortified."

"Well…" He took a small pause. "I mean, I wouldn't mind getting to know you. If you're all right with it, that is."

I froze in the midst of cutting up my steak, but resumed promptly without missing a beat. "Truthfully, I'm not really looking for anything right now."

"We could just be friends," he assured with a smile. "I'm not taking your mother too seriously on her scheme."

He was humorous and I appreciated it. We talked easily for the rest of the night. His earlier response to Mom made her quite careful with her words. I found out that Marcus Blight had a clinic a little over ten minutes away from my own place. His parents had retired to live in Wisconsin where the rest of his family was and would visit him every few months. He'd surprised them with the cruise after getting a promotion. It was very sweet.

"Think we'll bump into each other from now on?" he asked as they were getting ready to leave.

"I'm sure," was my polite reply. "We could do coffee over weekends."

"That would be great." He smiled. They all wished us farewell and headed toward their car.

Mrs. Blight made a point to hold my hand and kiss my cheek. "You're a wonderful young woman, Lilian. I can see you have worked very hard for your success."

She shook my hand firmly with the kindest look I'd ever received from anyone in my life. I tried not to tear up and thanked her. She then bid my mom a good evening and they were gone.

"So, what did you think?" she chirped as I moved away to gather my things to leave.

"If you want surgery, then use the money I send you," came my irritated reply. "I'm not looking to marry anyone for benefits."

"Lilian!" she hissed and grabbed my bicep to turn me around roughly. I snatched back my arm and stared her down. I was half a foot taller than her and didn't need to cower anymore. I didn't know what had gotten into me but something about the way Barbara spoke to me gave me a boost of confidence and suddenly I wasn't afraid to show that I was upset and tired of her antics.

"I only came here to spare you the embarrassment of them realizing you have a daughter that wants to keep you at a distance." I seethed. I could see her back away slightly at my statement. With a deep breath to smoothen out my glare, I threw my shawl around myself.

"You think *that* would've embarrassed me?" she shot back. "You walked in here in *that* dress looking like a slut!"

"Me? A slut?" I laughed out loud. "Remind me why Dad divorced you."

SMACK!

My cheek stung from the impact of her palm. It felt like I had been whacked with a pan, but I honestly didn't regret saying it one bit. It had been bubbling in my chest for quite a while.

"Let me remind you of your own value, Lilian," she spat. "All the things you did to bring Mark's wrath upon you."

"Mark abusing me was his own incompetence as a human being," I retorted, my voice dangerously calm. "Quite similar to yours in being a parent. I did nothing but love him and try to make him happy. But nothing I did was ever good enough for him, and the same can be said for you to this day."

"Watch your tongue with me!"

"You abandoned me, Mom." I scoffed. "You kicked me out when you found out he'd...he'd *raped* me and left me at his mercy for years. You let him abuse me for *years* until I almost died. That's the one time you remembered I was your daughter. That was the one night you truly gave a damn, didn't you?"

She stared at me silently with rage in her eyes. And I realized how much I resembled her when I looked in the mirror at the end of the day.

It broke me.

I picked up my bag and quickly walked toward the door, scooping up Holly on the way. Cotton whined sadly and Holly barked desperately for her friend. Mom yelled at me to come back, that it was too dark to drive but I ignored it. She pleaded for me to stay, that we could talk it out over dessert, that I barely ever came home. But I had gone deaf with the rage of my blood pumping behind my ears.

There was no home for me here.

Chapter 4

"Lilith, please pick up!" Aubrey whined over my landline's voicemail as I stirred myself some chocolate Nesquik. *"Jacque asked me out on a date, and I don't know what to say.* This is big news. Call me back!" She shrieked that last part.

I stared blankly at the wall as I stirred, Aubrey's voice entering one ear and going straight out the other. My mind was as blank as the wall. I needed to gather some thoughts in there, but what was I supposed to think? My mind had shut down. I'd slept well into the afternoon and had yet to even wash my face. I was so glad it was Sunday. By Monday, I would be up and pumping. But right now, I needed to relax.

Turning my head around, I had the unfortunate mental capacity to assess my physical state. My face looked dull and stale from over-oxidized foundation, and mascara-stained tear tracks down my cheeks. The eyeliner had spread around my eyes and inspired the inner raccoon to surface. I felt like a raccoon, too. Eating off-brand chips that tasted bland, drowned in soda, and watching horrible comedy movies late into the night as I'd cried.

I loved having the occasional mental breakdown.

Holly barked and I jumped out of my trance, spilling some chocolate milk on the marble tile. Holly licked it up immediately. I breathed deeply to feel a little alive, and inhaled the milk in one go.

Beep.

"Lilith, are you dead? Should I call the police?"

I ran toward the phone and accepted her call. "It's the weekend."

"Oh…I forgot. Did you hear that Jacq—"

I sighed. "Yes. Look, just be yourself with him. He's quite similar to you so I doubt he'd have a bad impression of you."

"How the hell am I supposed to do *that*?"

"What do you mean?" I raised a brow and placed the glass gently on a nearby table.

"I don't know…" She trailed off. "I just really like him and want to impress him. I'm not very impressive as a person."

"You're twenty-five with a Master's degree in Fashion and Jewelry. What on *earth* do you mean?"

"Who'd be interested in that? That's girly stuff."

I groaned, realizing that Aubrey had internalized a lot of misogyny from her exes and other men around her.

"The guy loves fashion, Aubrey." I rubbed my forehead. "Haven't you been through his Instagram?"

"What if he's better at fashion than me?"

"You have a *master's* degree," I shouted helplessly. "Good grief, Aubrey, do you really think dating is a good idea when the other person can't even get to know and like who you really are? You don't wanna show them that because you don't like yourself at all!"

"I-I *do* like myself!"

"Then why do you keep *changing* yourself for other people?" Silence lingered on the line for several moments. I sat back on the edge of my couch's backrest, waiting for her to respond. "Hello? Aubrey?"

"You're right…" she whispered. "I'll think on it."

Click.

Slight guilt tugged at my chest, and I knew I must've hurt her feelings a bit with that. But the way she acted was really getting on my nerves. It had been a year of deliberately undermining herself and being a doormat. Probably longer, which was why she came to me. I had tried improving it with subtle suggestions and directing her into considering therapy for her self-esteem and pattern of running after assholes, but it was time I was blunt with her.

With a groan, I let myself fall backward onto the couch. Holly jumped up on me, demanding pats and ruffles, which I was more than happy to give.

I had a very weird feeling that last night wasn't the last of the motherly drama left to deal with.

The phone rang once again, and I sighed in annoyance. Why didn't people understand that they should leave others alone during the weekends? I swung my arm over my eyes and ignored the sound bouncing around the room, until it finally stopped. And went to voicemail.

"Hi, it's Emily."

I froze.

"I don't want to pick a fight over the phone. Tell me when we can meet."

Did this have to happen today out of all times?

I needed to get out of here before the walls caved in and crashed over my head.

"I was surprised you called," Marcus said as we settled behind a table by the window in a quaint little coffee shop. "I wasn't expecting to see you again so soon."

"I know it's weird," I shook my head, "but I'm a really reserved person and don't know a lot of people so…"

"Oh." His eyes widened in confusion. "Sorry, that hardly sounds believable."

"I-it's true." I could feel my face go red with embarrassment. "I don't know why I thought of you off the bat, I just…maybe because your mom was really nice the other day, and so were you. It's rare to find people like that these days."

"If it's any comfort, I have trouble trusting people, too," he said with an understanding nod. The waitress came over, promptly took our order, and left. "Just black coffee? The apple pie's really nice here, by the way."

"I don't have a sweet tooth."

"You're full of surprises, Lilian."

"Lilith."

His eyes shone with curiosity, and it was kind of flattering, to be honest.

"Your name's Lilith?"

"I changed it after I moved out of my mom's place."

"Wow," he breathed. "You're really something. Why Lilith out of all names? It's close to the name your mom gave you."

"I just admired Lilith from the biblical stories a lot. I mean, I'm generally not a religious person but I never saw her as someone evil. She was just…normal and demonized for it."

"I agree with that interpretation." He nodded excitedly. "Have you heard the reinterpretation of Medusa's story and how the curse was actually a blessing in disguise?"

"I have!" I perked up. "The patriarchal system placed Athena in a position to punish Medusa who was a victim of Poseidon's assault, so in its guise she gave Medusa the power to protect herself by turning men to stone so they may harm her no more."

"It makes more sense that way," he agreed. "I'm obsessed with folklore, fairytales, and mythologies. I often look out for retellings that bring out aspects I wouldn't have noticed as a man. I guess I just got tired of reading the same thing over and over."

"What do you mean?"

"I mean, pick up whatever classic you can that's been a hit and written mostly by men. I found a repetition of gore, violence, and war in most. I was inspired to write a paper on this in high school when I found out that Disney had changed most of its classic animated movies to be more family friendly. It's kind of where my love of reading sprang from."

I listened, absolutely stunned and entranced as we discussed things back and forth about everything and anything under the sun. It was... exhilarating. I'd never been able to talk to anyone like this before, mostly because I never took the opportunity to seek out people like him. I'd always been so desperate to survive and leave my ex-boyfriend and Mom that I forgot I needed friends, too.

To be fair, I still had as many trust issues as I did back then, and everyone back in Michigan had been terrible to me. I wasn't even sure why I'd let my mom follow me to New York. Probably all the years of being gaslit had led me to feel responsible for her own terrible circumstances. I was only just beginning to accept that her behavior toward me was never justified under any circumstances.

Should I stop sending her money?

"About last night…" He interjected out of nowhere, and I suddenly felt myself growing alarmed. "I know what she said about your nose wasn't very nice. I hope you didn't mind me butting in the way I did. I understand that it was something for you to tackle on your own."

"What? No!" I cried out. "No, please don't apologize. No one's ever stood up for me like that. I was just shocked."

"I just wanted to make sure." He chuckled nervously. "Hopefully I wasn't being too forward. I was just stating a fact; you're incredibly beautiful."

"Thank you," I said awkwardly and sipped my coffee to hide my face. My chest felt warm again. It was a weird feeling and definitely not something I was used to. I knew paranoia would ruin it for me sooner or later. I could feel his gaze on me, soft and kind. I glanced at him, his eyes catching the sunlight. They were green. But I was sure they had looked brown last night.

I blinked and glanced away, concerned that my mental health was taking a toll on my memory. If it got too bad, I'd saved up enough to retire comfortably. Maybe if I could stretch my career another fifteen years, I wouldn't have to worry about the next generation, either—if that was ever a possibility of happening.

Next generation?

I was shocked at my own thoughts. I'd always actively avoided the topic of kids, especially after moving out. I always believed I could never be a mother or partner to anyone because of the abuse I'd put up with. I didn't want to perpetuate a never-ending cycle of generational trauma. I would kill myself before I ever inflicted that onto a child. Recovery from trauma was extremely difficult, and I was losing all hope of being okay anytime soon.

A prolonged but easy silence fell over us. I felt a lot calmer and my coffee was gone.

"I'm kind of taken aback." Marcus laughed lightly. "When we met your mom, she made you out to be this meek and tender thing that was always stressed and needed someone to desperately lean on all the time, but you're pulling through just fine from what I can see."

I wanted to laugh at him. Mom was right, but not in the way she thought. I did need someone. A therapist.

Yet, as I sat here, I realized that I could at least start out with a friend.

Chapter 5

Coffee with Marcus was great, but it was more than enough energy I had to expend on anyone today. I needed to be alone. And so, I found myself in Central Park on a nice bench by the lake, my journal in hand, tapping my pen against my temple.

Cut off Mother for good?

When to confront Emily?

Continue helping Aubrey?

Dinner?

"I gotta cut down on takeout." I sighed to myself and stared at the ducks squawking in the distance and getting in the lake.

"Decisions, decisions," came a dramatic sigh by my shoulder and I screamed, causing the ducks to screech and flutter their wings in panic, soaking any unfortunate passerby with a spray of water.

"Jesus Christ, Lilith!" Cristo gasped, having run away to the other side of the bench and grabbing his chest, but then he smirked. "Should I say those names in the same breath?"

I rolled my eyes as he straightened and stared up at the sky, making the sign of the cross and putting his palms together. My face felt warm, although I wasn't sure why.

"You think that's an apology enough for God?"

"What do you want, Cristo?"

"I just remembered God isn't the only one I have to apologize to." He grinned at me.

I gave him a dubious look.

Is this guy right in the head?

"You're totally judging me," he stated blankly and groaned while jabbing his hands into his pockets. "Look, I just wanted to apologize for yesterday. I shouldn't have dropped you."

"Better late than never, I guess..." I replied dismissively and put my journal away. "But why do I get the sense that you're stalking me?"

"Stalking you?" He chuckled and crossed his arms. He looked nice outside the formal events I normally saw him at. He was dressed in black fitted jeans and a black T-shirt, paired with a short-sleeved white button up left open. His Nike shoes were very…interesting. It hurt my eyes. A dark-gray backpack hung on his shoulder, hair casually parted to the side, and he was even wearing round glasses. Very nerdy.

It was kind of cute.

Extremely cute, actually.

"We could've done this on Monday in my office. Not in the middle of the day at Central Park."

"I was on my way to the orphanage site, Lilith." He rolled his eyes, smirking. "I saw you and decided to take a future task off my agenda. Anyway, if I had to stalk someone, it would be the construction manager."

"I wasn't aware you swung that way."

"I swear to god you're just fucking with me at this point," he deadpanned, but sighed and dropped down next to me. "I suspect him of overestimating the funds to rake in some illicit gains."

He was sitting rather close, almost touching my shoulder. My heart rate spiked from his proximity, which was a little confusing, because what the hell could *that* mean? His presence shouldn't do that to me.

The breeze carried his cologne over to me and he smelled rather nice. Like freshly mown grass. I looked over at him, a little confused that such a male scent existed until I noticed grass stains on his sleeves. Had he been rolling around on the ground?

"And that's why you're dressed like a teenage TikToker in broad daylight?"

He stared at me from beneath his glasses perched low on his nose, stormy gray eyes piercing into my soul quite literally and making my heart skip a beat. "I'll take that as a compliment, thank you very much."

"Very convincing cover." I shook my head and looked away, trying to hold back my smile. What was with him, and why was he being like this? I didn't want to give him the satisfaction of seeing me laugh in the slightest. I knew I should let things go for his stupidity yesterday, but I had a hard time not holding grudges.

Once upon a time, I was too forgiving a person and look where that had landed me...

"Hey, umm…" he exhaled nervously, "I never apologized for what happened all those years ago. Not properly, at least. I was a dumb kid and should've just gone along with the session. I heard you failed the assignment."

I almost snapped my neck turning to look at him. "How do you know that?"

"I've been in touch with Mrs. Beaumont for a while." He shrugged cheekily. "Don't tell my parents, though, please. They'll blow up on me for keeping secrets."

"Whoa, wait, does that mean you were in touch with the Dupont kids, too?"

"You already know them," he said in a cheerful tone as he pushed himself to stand. "Just…don't tell Mrs. Beaumont about that. Or my parents. Getting my dad's family back together was…totally not my scheme."

"I'm guessing *The Parent Trap* is your favorite movie."

"You're frighteningly insightful. Good day!"

Cristo rushed off, leaving me alone on the bench feeling extremely confused.

I muttered under my breath, "What the fuck?"

The loneliness was so overwhelmingly loud when I walked inside the house around sunset. It emanated from the walls quite literally. The apartment, although a small studio, felt so big. Usually, this would weigh on my chest and make me feel like I couldn't breathe, but I kept thinking about the park. And laughing.

I was kind of funny, wasn't I?

While the walls decorated with paintings and shelves still complained about the emptiness in the air, it didn't feel so obvious anymore. I'd had a pretty good day with both Marcus and Cristo.

As I walked toward the phone and played the voicemail on reflex, I knew nothing in that moment could take today's satisfaction away from me.

"Lilian, please pick up the phone. I'm so sorr—"

Beep.

Nothing at all, I thought as I shut off my mother's voice immediately.

Chapter 6

I hated myself for being there, but honestly, I wasn't sure where else to go.

Therapy, a snide part of myself remarked, but I shook it off. Alex was a good person, understood things and made sure I never dropped off the edge. I was as scared of medication as I was of drugs and Alex was the only barrier between us. I wouldn't trust anyone else to supply me and keep watch while I consumed it. Alex was trustworthy.

The door swung open and I could smell the smoke already.

"Aye, Lucifer!"

"Lilith," I grumbled. "Why do you *always* forget?"

"When it hits that good"—She rolled the joint between her fingers—"you don't need good memory."

I forgot to mention that I had only ever *attempted* to do drugs once, but I chickened out and ran away. Alex had laughed about it for weeks. I rolled my eyes at her laugh, a deep rumble from her belly. If it wasn't for her long, messy brown hair, she could've easily been mistaken for a teenage boy with that voice of hers.

But really, though, she had a terrible memory. Maybe I should just turn away now.

"Ahh, you're chickening out again." She smirked.

"Am *not*."

"Come on in." She swung the door wide open. "I made edibles."

Knowing I'd cornered myself into this, I sighed and entered her place. It was beyond me why she made her space look like an acid trip: neon colors splashed onto the walls in spirals and zigzags, an assortment of indigenous masks decorated the only plain black wall, peculiar chandeliers (a little messy from the necklaces she'd throw at them), and bright bean bags and furry rugs. A warm hearth blazed in the corner of the room, and the mantel was loaded with snow globes. Alex's place was the epitome of maximalism.

"Listen, before we start"—I grabbed her wrist—"I appreciate how highly you think of me and getting me clients, but you need to stop misinforming them. I'm not cupid."

"Is this about Aubrey?"

"She's completely changing the way I work now! She was fine until a few days ago."

Alex snickered and plopped down onto a bean bag. "Look, I just wanted her off my back. Sorry to use you as a scapegoat. But you do catch vibes, though."

"*Patterns*," I grumbled and sat next to her on a cushion. "What have you got?"

"I've been making gummy bears," she said and reached out for a jar full of jewel-toned jellies. I looked at it carefully as she held the jar in front of me with an encouraging gaze. "You know I'll take care of you. We're friends, aren't we?"

I glanced up at her with guilt in my heart, realizing I'd negated her position in my life a lot. She was always there whenever I broke down and tried something stupid. I'd always kept her at arm's length without realizing how closely she held me to herself. Enough to make sure I'd never be successful in my bizarre attempts to end my life. I wasn't like that anymore, of course, but it must've been exhausting for her. I felt like such a terrible person for always treating her as a mere acquaintance when she had acted as so much more.

"You deserve a little fun, Lilith." She nudged my arm. "I don't mind you crying, but it's time you appreciated the good stuff that comes with life, too. Go on."

Eyeing the jar of colorful little bears, I took a deep breath and moved before my anxiety could paralyze me. I popped a gleaming green jelly in my mouth and chewed on it. It tasted different, but not bad. It was still sweet.

And we sat there and talked, until thirty minutes later, it kicked in. A slight buzz that was...kind of nice. I expected to be dizzy, throwing up, or crying but this was nice. A warm feeling in my chest that made me realize things weren't all that bad. I had Holly, Alex, and Marcus. I had a nice job and a pretty apartment I could only dream of at eighteen. I only had to work four days a week. Hell, I had my own company!

I took another gummy bear and popped it in my mouth, revelations from the universe and Mother Earth coming to me as I realized that I couldn't be happy all the time but I couldn't be sad forever, either. My life was like a rainbow sherbet from Baskin Robbins: sometimes weird and too sour but also pleasant at times.

The swirls and jagged lines on the walls started to pulsate lightly with a neon glow. I reached for another gummy, but my hand was smacked away.

"That's enough for right now." Alex chuckled, and so did I.

I laid back and stared up at the ceiling as bizarre as the walls, taking in the chandelier that seemingly broke apart and floated around gently. It was nice and peaceful. It was fun.

Alex's phone rang and she picked it up immediately. "Jesus Christ, my man, it's you! Yeah, I have your stash, come by. You're almost here? Great."

She hung up and I watched her rummaging around the table, searching for the package for her customer.

"You know, I should get going."

"In this state?" She shook her head. "You'll chase after the lights and walk straight into traffic. If you need to be home right now, then I'll drive you."

"I want to take a walk."

"You can do that in your complex's garden," she suggested, finally finding a small square package and tossing it in her hands. The bell rang and she pulled me up to stand. "I'll drop you off. Come on."

I stretched my hands out to her and she grabbed them, pulling me up to stand, and my head spun slightly. I giggled and swayed, grabbing onto Alex's biceps to step into my shoes properly. She reached out to open the door.

"You know, Alex," I giggled, "if you ever wanna get married—"

"I'll shoot myself in the leg before I ever agree to that." She laughed and swung the door open. "Jesus!"

"John!"

"Cristo?" I gawked, suddenly sober. "Alex, do you know everyone in New York?"

"Only the best people."

"And for the best stash." Cristo grinned, handing Alex an envelope. "Thanks again for this. You did a lot on such short notice."

"It's nothing."

They exchanged hands and bumped fists.

"I didn't think you were the fun type, Lilith." He smirked. "Is the stress finally getting to you?"

"None of your business." I rolled my eyes.

"Huh. I bet it's why your memory's failing you these days?"

"Lay off her." Alex chuckled. "I need to drop her home right now, so is there anything else you need?"

"Nah, this is all."

Cristo cocked his head and studied me curiously. I only crossed my arms and looked away, feeling my face flush from the intoxication and his intense look.

"Wait." He smirked again. "This is your first time, isn't it?"

"Cristo," I shot back warningly.

Alex gave me an odd look and pushed at Cristo, urging him to leave. He seemed to understand her gaze and hurriedly turned to go.

"I gotta be somewhere real quick. See you next week! Nice meeting you, Lilith."

No different from yesterday, he scurried off.

"Do I scare him?" I turned to Alex.

She gave me a dubious expression, as if unsure how to respond. "You tell me, Lucifer." She shook her head and closed the door behind her, locking it and grabbing my arm to lead me away.

The next morning was strangely peaceful. I didn't feel agitated, or down in the dumps, or stressed about the next hour. For the first time in my entire life, I wasn't planning ahead or stuck in the past. I was focused on the present, and not only as a distraction.

Running my gaze over the files, I matched a potential partner to thirty-five-year-old Ibiza Prices, a furniture designer, and a major shareholder in many companies. His name was Maurice Grover, forty, a big part of the agriculture industry in Europe and sitting on loads of intergenerational wealth. I'd assessed him once myself at a premier for *World War Z*. The guy was obsessed with zombies and had a room with arcade games of *House of Dead*, all editions. Good dude.

I picked up my phone and shot her an e-mail, subsequently returning to my paperwork.

A knock came at the glass door of my office. I gestured for them to come in, still focused on reading the files.

"You've been invited to Barry Halls' wedding. It's next weekend," Lyra, my assistant, announced. "He's asked you to profile his younger sister and hopefully find her a match."

"The girl's a free spirit, Lyra." I shook my head. "She'll never settle, and she will definitely not agree to this."

"He's asking for a discreet service."

"I'm not a spy." I laughed. "Figure out if she doesn't already know me before I make a fool of myself in front of her."

"All right."

I went back to work, entering data into my laptop quickly. It had only been a few seconds when she knocked again.

I gestured her in. "That was quick of you." I said.

"Were you expecting me?"

I jumped at the familiar deep voice with a yelp, and the man fell back into the loveseat behind him in shock.

"Marcus!"

"You scare easily," he breathed out with a hand to his heart. "And I mean that in all ways possible."

"I would've appreciated a call!" I hissed, reaching up to fix my glasses hanging off an ear. He was wearing dark pants and a vest under his lab coat, holding a familiar paper bag in one hand. "Is that…coffee?"

"Uh, yeah…" He trailed off with a slight blush on his face. "I was on a break and thought that maybe I could drop by and say hi. Ask how you're doing."

I glanced at the clock, shocked at how time had flown and how much I'd gotten done without realizing.

"That's nice of you." I smiled and got up to sit next to him. He handed me my coffee, and we talked aimlessly about our days as I tried to ignore the sly looks my employees were sending me from outside my office.

"Is everything all right?" he said abruptly after a short silence.

"Yeah, it's just…" I laughed lightly, "my employees. They, uhh, they're placing bets right now."

"Oh?"

"They're too invested in my lack of a love life." I rolled my eyes. "It's such a mystery to them why I don't date."

"In all honesty, you're a very mysterious woman." He said this so seriously, I almost choked on my coffee.

Sputtering, I shook my head and chugged down a sip to clear my throat. "No, I'm not!"

"Really? What's your major, then?"

"Genetics."

He paused, genuinely surprised. "Are you serious?"

"It's very important when assessing couples who plan on having children."

"And that's not supposed to surprise me?"

I thought on it, comparing myself to others in my mentorship. "Fair point."

"How did you even end up in this industry?" He shook his head, seeming genuinely confused.

"It's a funny story, really." I laughed. "Halfway into my second year, I wrote a paper on how behaviors and personalities correlated to genes that could make it possible to create a system that predicts and identifies suitable matches, either emotional or reproductive. I then became obsessed with it and created said system with a team. Then word got around and some seniors came to help improve on it and tested it out. One of them wanted to test their compatibility with her husband and it was pretty low, which caused a fight. And then Mrs. Beaumont came up to me after saying that she'd predicted it well before my machine did. I'm not sure how I became so interested in what she did, but she gave me her number to call and…it just felt like the right thing to do. Probably because I saw the money it made and really needed it at the time."

"But you've been doing this for quite a while," he said. "You're only thirty, right?"

"Yeah, I mentored under her while completing my studies. Had to leave one of my jobs and also take up summer courses to graduate early. Then I just became lucky to incorporate my studies that started all this into my business. It's what helped with the popularity, or I would've crashed in the first few years without it. I paid off all my loans immediately and the rest is now mine."

"You've worked very hard," he said and sat quietly in contemplation. "My life was very comfortable and not as interesting. It feels like I haven't accomplished much."

"You're a doctor that makes people more comfortable in their bodies." I shrugged and took a light sip. "I think you're doing an impressive job."

"It feels like such a crime, though." He sighed. "Living a comfortable life and having everything handed to me on a plate. I do give back as much as I can, but so many people struggle, and it turns them into such interesting personalities."

"Trust me," my voice fell grim, "only about half of them make it out alive with not much accomplished, and even lesser into a successfully comfortable life. Struggle isn't…it isn't…I don't know how to say it. It isn't beautiful. It's hard and breaks you down really bad sometimes."

"I think I might've romanticized it," he said apologetically. "I'm sorry."

"You're a heck of a lot more self-aware than most people in your place," I said. "Maybe if more people were as empathic and selfless, it would make living easier."

"I get that." He nodded, and we fell into a comfortable silence. It wasn't long before it was time for him to leave. He walked out with a smile and a casual "see you later." I masked my face in politeness, although internally attacked with memories of everything I had gone through to get where I was.

I would kill to be Marcus right now.

Chapter 7

Aubrey sat patiently before me, but the annoyance rolled off of her in waves. I wondered if it was directed at me, and I wouldn't blame her because our last conversation hadn't been the nicest.

"I…" she started, but paused and breathed deeply, "I stopped seeing him."

"Is it okay if I ask why?"

She seemed nervous, fiddling with her thumbs as if she had a secret too big to bear. Her eyes were red, nose puffy, and cheeks bright with freckles. Aubrey was not okay.

"I'm so tired, Lilith," she whispered while staring blankly at her hands. "So, *so* tired of not feeling what I want to. What I should."

"And what *should* you feel?" I tried to sound kind. Honestly, I wasn't sure what to expect besides more recklessness and demand on her part. I was only here because she paid me for this meeting. As sad as that sounded, that's just how business worked.

At least that's how *I* worked.

Maybe I had deep-set issues related to money that I should've been looking into. Either way, I had to try to care about Aubrey's feelings. Surprisingly, I didn't have to put in much effort because deep down, I understood where she was coming from.

"I know books and movies aren't the best place to look for what romance is like but," She sighed, "I was talking to a friend yesterday and… it was just the way he talked about her and the way he looked at her when she came to pick him up…"

"Oh…"

Yeah, I knew what she felt.

"It felt like I was watching a movie about the two of them." She twiddled her thumbs, teeth digging into her bottom lip. "For some reason, I feel like I can never have that. My heart's never, like…fluttered with anyone, and I've never been able to be myself around people."

"Why is it so important for you to be with someone right now?" I asked gently, reaching over to touch her knuckles with delicate fingers. "You have so much to live for, you know?"

"Like what?"

"Well, when's the last time you designed something?" I prodded while racking my brain for her profile that was snugly put away in the second drawer of my office. "I remembered you having a really successful fashion show in Dubai two years ago. Why haven't you done anything since?"

"My boyfriend at the time felt it was too much pressure to date someone that well known." She shrugged and pulled away to chip at a cookie on her plate. "Said I was susceptible to cheat when I had so many rich men with their eyes on me."

I was stunned and shocked but realized that I'd almost done the same thing to please Mark back when I was dating him. I'd almost dropped my full-ride scholarship to college because he was so sure I would cheat when I left. Luck had been in my favor, though…but not in the way I expected.

Shaking my head lightly, I pushed away the horrid memory and focused back onto Aubrey who had decided to try dipping her cookie into her coffee.

"I think you need another fashion show, Aubrey," I said in all seriousness.

"What." She blanked out and dropped her cookie. Coffee droplets splashed onto the mahogany table, and I wondered if she'd given up on herself enough to never reconsider such a thing.

"I said what I said."

"Lilith…" she began slowly as if talking to a toddler, "do you not understand how long it takes to build a reputation in the fashion world? And I just…dropped out! I'm not relevant anymore."

"And what does that matter?" I gave a nonchalant shrug. "Bring your friends over, make them try it on, have a good day. I'm not asking you to go big, I'm asking you to go home. Where your heart is."

Aubrey sat before me in stunned silence, and I felt so sorry for her. Had she truly forgotten herself to such an extent? How much had she changed herself over the course of a few years just to please men that could never truly love her?

"I don't know if I have it in me."

"I guess you need to start going to a few fashion shows and be inspired again." The words spilled out of my mouth as a matter-of-fact reply. I wondered where I was getting all the right things to say so confidently. Admittedly, maybe I really wanted Aubrey to be okay again and it wasn't just because of being paid. She was such a nice person, if only a little clueless.

She stood up abruptly, determination on her face. "I'll do it!"

"Right now?" was my bewildered response. Her face fell and she plopped back down.

"No, not right now." She sighed. "I have some things to take care of by the end of the week, but I'll book the ticket for it right here and now." She quickly pulled out her phone and tapped away. "I can't give myself a moment to be distracted or forget about this."

I chuckled as genuine warmth and adoration flooded my chest. "I'm glad you're getting a head start."

We got up to leave after I was done sipping my coffee. She'd booked her ticket, and I could see her skin practically buzzing with excitement. We walked out of the store to part ways, but she grabbed my hands before I could leave.

"Lilith"—She squeezed my fingers between hers, eyes shining—"you…you come off pretty strong sometimes but…it's done me a lot of good. You're probably the only honest person I have in my life. Thank you."

I smiled and patted her hand. "You're a good person, Aubrey. I have faith in you."

With that, I gave her a small wave and walked off.

Tugging my coat tighter around myself, I picked up my pace. My heels clacked on the sidewalk, and I felt my toes cramp up in my wedges. It was getting colder.

Somehow the only ones that seemed immune to the shift in temperatures were kids. As I walked on the familiar strip that surrounded Central Park, I could hear their squeals and laughter carrying faintly in the wind. I guessed I could use a walk through the park, seeing as how draining my meeting was with Aubrey.

I pondered it as my foot sank slightly into the grass, walking to find my familiar spot by the pond. Aubrey had spent far too long dating all the wrong people, so it was only natural she should take a break. Was there a thing called being single for too long? Thinking back on my own dating life, I had only ever dated three men seriously. Mark was the worst, and I hadn't dated since being set free from his torment. I did feel alone, but after all he had put me through, it was the only safe choice.

Mark wasn't my only abusive ex. The other two guys I'd dated hadn't been much different, but it was more subtle abuse. Subliminal, emotional, manipulative. Mark was outright violent.

After him, I decided that my luck was just too terrible when it came to love.

Is that why I did this job? Perhaps in a way, I was looking out for women and making sure they didn't get trapped with the wrong guy. That's why people hired me, didn't they? To see if I could make happily ever after possible for them. I'd had a good run so far, with only two marriages ending in divorce, but only because the parties were forced into it.

Living for years on my own had made me so used to being independent, but it was becoming so tiring and draining. I wanted to be taken care of for a change.

Was that too much to ask?

I didn't realize how lost in thought I was until the laughter grew louder. Children shrieking and yelling, seemingly fighting over crayons and colored pencils as they ran around a wooden picnic table. A woman stood at the end of the table, annoyed and impatient. I could tell she was minutes away from shouting. I watched mindlessly as a child got up with their sheet of paper and ran off to the swings where a man stood and pushed them as they laughed.

Wait a second…

I blinked, wondering if I was seeing things right. Was that really Cristo?

Should I have felt annoyed? I felt annoyed. I wasn't sure why but…being around Cristo just…

Threatens my bubble?

As much as I hated to admit it to myself, it was true. He didn't do much, but his simple and harmless existence was pushing at buttons I didn't know I had, and it made me panic. Seeing him playing with kids, smiling at them, and carrying them around…it was cute. And I hated how attracted to him I felt in that moment.

Turning on my heel, I marched off quickly as I pushed down the vomit-inducing tenderness springing up in my chest. No, I didn't need this. I didn't need any of this right now. I couldn't be around someone like this only to realize they were going to be just as terrible as the rest. As much as

I would've liked being friends with him, I knew deep down it couldn't happen.

Feeling the things I felt when I was with him repulsed me. And that was a problem.

"Lilith!"

My face burned hot and I quickened my pace, but I knew it would be no use. He'd already run up and jogged lightly next to me with a stupid grin on his face. "Is it fair to assume you're the one stalking me today?"

I halted abruptly in my tracks to shoot him a glare. "I wasn't!"

"You're pretty far away from your favorite pond."

"It's not my favorite." I rolled my eyes and started walking again.

He followed, jamming his hands into his windbreaker's pockets. His eyes travelled around the park, peering back over his shoulder as more laughter erupted.

"I guess Trisha can handle them," he mumbled unsurely.

"What are you even doing out here with kids?" I asked suspiciously. "Are you a part-time nursery teacher?"

"They're from an orphanage nearby." He chuckled. "I'm getting ideas from them."

"How are kids supposed to help?"

"Well, they're my clients, aren't they?"

He wasn't wrong…

"Anyway, I don't think kids are asked enough about what they want to see when they walk around the city." He shrugged and fell into step with me despite having longer strides.

"It's not like that's necessary. They stay inside and play video games all day."

"Why do you think they do that?"

I sighed in defeat, seeing his point.

"I mean," he began, "you do match-making, so don't you have to consider whether the people you set up are going to be good parents?"

That made me feel a little guilty. I'd only ever thought of kids as something to help carry forward their parents' work, which was why I was more focused in the best gene make-up rather than how they'd be treated as individuals regardless of it. Admittedly, it was tone-deaf of me to do so, seeing as how I'd grown up with a terrible parent myself.

Years ago, I promised myself I'd never be the kind of parent she was, but I lost the kid before I could even try. Then again, I knew I could never be a mother with the environment and state of mind I was in back then. I would've aborted it myself had Mark and his mother not... Jesus.

Speaking of motherhood, I needed to talk to Emily already. I knew it was about the case I filed against the two. Emily, Mark's mother, was complicit in the abuse. An enabler, and even took part in it verbally, if not physically. She allowed him a space where he was free to do what he wanted and it was horrifying that she, as a woman, participated in it and stood by to watch it all happen to me.

"Hello?" Cristo waved his hand in front of my face and I pushed it away with a finger, shaking my head. He'd interfered too much without meaning to and I hated it.

"I need to go," I said as gently as possible and picked up my pace, leaving him in the dust.

"You know *what*?" he yelled. "I wish you wouldn't leave me hanging all the time!"

I rolled my eyes, not even bothering to respond. Verbally, at least.

Not my problem, Cristo.

Chapter 8

It was a cold Tuesday evening, but the restaurant was pleasantly warm. *Emily*. Silky brown hair throwing off gold light, center parted, slicked down over the scalp, and clipped back with a pretty brooch. Lips too pink, and eyes too warm for someone who'd let me suffer for years under her son's thumb. She sat down before me, her skin paler than I remembered. The deep purple dress stood out starkly against her complexion.

Oh, no fake tan today.

"The ring's nice," I commented with a sip of my wine.

"His name's George," she said carelessly. "He has great taste, doesn't he?"

"Acquired?" I said, boring my eyes into hers.

Her gaze was sharp. "You've gotten brave."

"Better than being desperate." I set my wine down gently. "Don't want anything ruining your big day, I assume?"

"It's been years, Lilian."

She sounded so casual and dismissive.

"You think invalidating my pain will get you anywhere?"

The waiter arrived, asking for our orders. Emily didn't have the chance to stare me down as she turned to him with a smile and ordered a Coho salmon with a side of creamed baby spinach.

"Just water for a drink, please," she added.

He turned to me. "And for you?"

I smiled at him. "What do you suggest, André?"

"We have a new crab recipe with a side of grilled fruit."

"I'll have that, then. Thank you."

He left with a polite smile, and I could only wish he'd rubbed off some positive energies onto

Emily when she opened her mouth. "Quite popular with the men now, I see."

"I respect the working class in general," I shot back. "They're really nice when you're not trying to get them fired."

"You really can't let go of the past." She sneered through gritted teeth.

"No." I laughed. "You're just worried about it catching up with you. Have you been hiding it well?"

"I don't see why you can't drop it and move on."

"What's hard about showing up to court, Emily?" I taunted. "Is it too far of a drive for you? I didn't see you making the same excuse when it came to Mark's accident."

"Mark's death does not concern you anymore," she said in controlled softness.

"It's so easy playing the victim for you, isn't it?" I smiled mockingly. "Isn't that why he joined the police force?"

Her eyes started tinting with red as a sheen came to them. "He did it to protect me."

"To legally help you get away with abuse," I pointed out.

"We didn't know better!"

"And yet you keep your son's confederate flag."

She shut up as André set down the water, pouring her a glass.

"Your food will arrive in ten minutes," he informed us and took his leave.

"I can't stand another minute with you," Emily muttered and reached out for her water.

"I had to put up with you guys beating me for years." I scrunched my nose at her. "You'll be fine."

Her fingers tightened around her glass, the elaborate engagement ring throwing off speckles of light as she moved to drink. She set her glass down and I took the chance to curate some silence, reaching for my phone to scroll through.

Emily's gaze wandered around the place, studying the people around her.

I wondered how long she could keep it up. I watched her acrylic nails tap rhythmically against the table, the clinking of glasses and utensils on plates interrupted my aimless thoughts,

"You should probably look into getting married and actually living instead of being fixated on the past," she advised, feigning whatever little kindness she could. "What Mark did was awful, but you can't hold me responsible for his actions."

"He's dead," I agreed, "but you're in court for your own faults. Have you forgotten so easily? How you killed your own grandchild?"

"That was not my son's child," she snapped a little too loudly.

The restaurant wasn't too crowded, but it did grab some people's attention nearby. She cleared her throat lightly, but I sat without a care in the world, elbow on the table and chin resting on my palm with my eyes trained on her steadily. She wasn't as scary as I believed she was all those years ago. She couldn't hurt me anymore. Mark was dead, and nothing she pulled could make me give up on the case.

André finally arrived with our food.

"Why are you in New York, Emily?" I asked with a concealed smirk. "Just for me?"

Her eyes narrowed dangerously on me. "I have important people to visit."

"Mark's father is very important." I nodded importantly and dug into my food. "Is he invited to the wedding?"

The shock on her face was priceless. She was an idiot for thinking I wouldn't do my research.

"How *dare* you—" she hissed but I held a hand up, cutting her off.

"No, it's all right. I understand you needed his emotional support after the funeral. I just didn't think sex came with it. Did my pregnancy remind you of your own guilt, Emily?"

"You shut your vile mouth!"

"But he wasn't even Mark's real father, though." I shook my head. "What a shame it would be if he found out."

"And you have evidence?"

"Wouldn't you like to know?" I smirked.

I saw Emily's hand reach for her half-full glass of water, ready to throw it at me.

"*Oh!*" Her screech made me jump as André tripped beside her, spilling an opened bottle of wine onto her. "*Jesus!*"

Emily's face was absolutely priceless and poor André apologized profusely, although he didn't appear very sorry. He winked at me discreetly as he reached out for tissues and dabbed at the tablecloth. I smacked a hand over my mouth before I could laugh. There was an abrupt jerk at my bicep, and I was promptly pulled out of the restaurant. I caught myself before I could yell out, seeing the hand attached as none other than Cristo Alexakis-Caron himself as we threaded through the tables and chairs.

My face was flaming as heat picked up in the rest of my body under his touch. "What in God's name—"

"You can't take God's name; you're Lilith," he said pointedly as we passed through the restaurant gates.

I snatched my arm and smacked his hand. He only pouted, cradling his hand gently.

"How do you always end up wherever I am?" I demanded loudly.

"Hmm." A thoughtful look came over his face. "What if it's a sign from the universe?"

"Oh, come off it!" I grunted and fixed my rings. Quick footsteps neared us, and I turned around, sighing in relief at the sight of Marcus approaching.

"Lilia—I mean, Lilith. Sorry. You okay?"

"I'm fine," I replied. "What brings you here?"

"I was having dinner with my cousins and saw the whole fiasco. Here."

He handed me my purse and phone, and I gave him a grateful look. "Thank you."

"Small world, huh?" Cristo commented, and I just rolled my eyes.

"Don't you have somewhere to be?"

"Hey, I saved your ass!" He sounded a little upset. "I mean, André did, but I gave him the idea."

Sighing, I rolled my eyes and turned to him. The look in his eyes made me feel guilty. I knew he was trying to conceal it, but I think my demeanor really was hurting him. It wasn't like he knew why I was being so cold toward him. Hell, even I didn't really know.

I glanced away toward the restaurant window, staring at a distraught and embarrassed Emily. She seemed so defeated and small.

It wouldn't have been possible without him.

"Thank you, Cristo," I said gently, giving him a small smile. "You really looked out for me today."

He was taken aback a bit.

"Oh, uhh, sure yeah, it was nothing." He grinned and I pinched him.

"You literally just—"

"Lilith," Marcus sounded serious behind me, "you've had a long evening. Should I take you home?"

My gaze darted to him, and then to Cristo. The light was bouncing off his golden skin, bringing out the marvelous sculpt of his cheeks and jaw. His eyes were a deep silver like the coat of a wizened wolf, warm and safe. He stood expectantly, but his smile said otherwise. He was ready to leave me be if I wanted or go with me if I stayed by him.

To be honest, I had the weirdest urge to stick around him. But…

"You're right," I turned to Marcus, "I have a busy day tomorrow." Hooking my arm around his elbow, I gave Cristo an apologetic look. He only smiled at me and bid us farewell, taking his leave. Marcus and I turned to walk away.

I did my best not to look back.

Chapter 9

The keys jingled as I unlocked the door.

"I don't know why but I was expecting a huge place." Marcus chuckled as we stepped inside. I shed my coat and tossed it onto the stand.

"It's just me." I sighed and kicked my heels off. "So it doesn't make sense to have too large a place."

"The interior's impeccable, though."

"I definitely made a big investment in it," I agreed. "Make yourself at home. Do you like mint lemonade?"

"Sure."

I went into the kitchen quickly without another word, really needing to be away from Marcus. My social battery felt like it would die out completely if I spent another second around him. It would've been nice to know he was such a talker. Not that it was a problem, honestly, but there was only so much I could handle after everything that had happened tonight.

My gaze dropped to the brown file on the island and I almost groaned. Emily's profile. Snatching it off the marble surface, I pulled open the trash drawer and stuffed it in. Sliding it shut, I breathed deeply and shook it off my mind. I didn't need that file anymore. If I did, I had a back-up copy at the office.

Spending time with Marcus seemed much more appealing now, and it would likely take my mind off of everything else going on, everything I had no desire to think about at present.

"You don't watch movies much, I guess?" he called out.

"Not really," I admitted, "I'm more of a reader. How'd you know?"

"Well, you don't have Netflix. Wanna watch something?"

"Sure. I'll get the popcorn."

A few minutes later, we sat comfortably on the couch with mint lemonade and fresh popcorn.

"Any preference?"

"Honestly, you go ahead and choose," I said and rose to my feet. "I'll change into something comfortable in the meantime."

He nodded and I left, feeling my heart pounding in my chest. I wasn't sure if I was overreacting, but something was different in the air around him. Not in a bad way, but I could smell something coming. I didn't want to expect it but, he did help me get home, and I did invite him in.

Ugh, I shook my head and locked the door to change into my pajamas. Nothing fancy, just a gray silk set with thin white stripes. They were my comfort pajamas, especially if I had a rough crying session coming on.

Did I have one coming on? It was better to be prepared.

I found myself back on the couch, sipping my lemonade as a horror movie played on the screen. It was only ten minutes into it and a dead little girl made an appearance. I giggled at the characters' screaming that followed it.

"You don't get scared?"

"What's so scary about this?" I shot back in amusement.

"I mean, they're clearly going to die."

"Everyone dies, Marcus." I rolled my eyes. "Plus, the movie isn't even remotely relatable."

"That's…hmm."

I waited for a moment, but he had nothing to say.

"I'm enjoying it, though," I assured him. "The production's great. It would be funnier if it was crappy CGI from the '90s."

"It made the stories better, though," he pointed out, and I nodded excitedly as we forgot the movie and delved into conversation about anything and everything once again.

It had been an hour of us laughing and chattering away, and I hadn't noticed how close we'd gotten to each other. I wasn't really noticing anything because of how comfortable we were, and there hadn't been any expectations of where this would go to begin with. When he lifted his hand to swipe away a piece of popcorn from the corner of my mouth, I couldn't bring myself to stop him from leaning in to kiss me.

His lips gently pressed against mine, and I sat frozen, not really knowing what to do. He pulled away for just a moment before he kissed me again, his hand going to the back of my head. I parted my lips slightly to kiss him back, hand going to his knee. It felt…nice.

I'd long accepted not to expect the butterflies and volcano explosions that the books talked about when it came to love and affection. Nice was fine.

Nice was enough.

It's the bare minimum, my conscience was surprisingly snarky, but I pushed it to the back of my head. I could deal with it another time. I hadn't had a kiss in an exceptionally long time, and I wanted to enjoy it.

His lips moved against mine intensely, hands sliding around my thighs to pull me onto his lap. I complied without hesitation and straddled him.

"Oh," I gasped, staring at him, feeling a flush creeping into my face.

"Too soon?"

"Could we…take it slow for now?" I suggested.

He smiled at me softly. "All right."

I leaned in to kiss him again, letting his hand rub up and down my side, and the other slipped into my hair to tilt my head.

This is nice, I thought.

His phone rang abruptly, startling us.

"Ah, shit," he muttered under his breath and reached for the phone on the side table. "It's my alarm. I'm supposed to start getting ready for bed."

"You have a curfew?" I smirked.

A defeated sigh left him. "And a surgery to perform first thing in the morning."

"We can't have that going wrong," I said and moved to get off of him.

He grabbed my hand before I could stand and drew me down, hand around my waist. His lips pressed against mine and I sighed, kissing him back for just a moment. I pushed myself off in the next second and pulled him to stand.

"I've got work, too." I reminded him. "Come on, off you go."

He chuckled and picked up his stuff as I cleared the space. Walking him to the door, I wondered if this was enough for me. A nice guy who cared. In all honesty, he seemed more of a best friend than boyfriend material to me, but it wasn't like we were making anything official.

Right?

How did this dating thing work again? God, it had been so long, it was as if I'd forgotten. Was I even ready to date?

I closed the door behind him and leaned my back against it with a huge sigh.

"What are you doing?" I whispered to myself.

Chapter 10

"Lilith!" came Aubrey's excited squeal as she ran into my office and plopped down onto the seat before my desk. Normally, I'd be quite annoyed, but today I felt all right. "You'll never guess what happened!"

"Not until you tell me, no," I agreed as I typed away and scanned the data for issues. "Make it quick, though. I have to leave for an appointment in ten minutes."

"I got invited to Fashion Week in South Korea!" she shrieked, jumping around in her seat

"Oh, wow, that's wonderful." I smiled at her. "The getaway you've been looking for, right?"

She smacked her hands on the table. "Yes, and I'm taking *all* my friends with me."

"That sounds like a lot of fun!"

"It *will* be!" she cheered. "You're coming with me!"

I blinked at her, trying to register what she said.

"Aubrey, I'm not—"

"Please?" She rose from her seat and reached across my desk to grab my hands. "You never take a break from work except on the weekends. It'll be *fun*. And South Korea's amazing with so many other conventions happening, you don't have to attend Fashion Week entirely."

"Well." I sighed, but she was right. I'd always wanted to travel but had never even left the country. South Korea sounded like a nice place to go to. My life had always been consumed with just working and then heading home to sleep. "There's a wedding I have to attend next weekend."

"Barry Halls, right? Mom and Dad are going, too. We'll be back by next Thursday!"

I calculated it in my head. Today was Wednesday, which meant we'd be leaving tomorrow. I wished she'd given me a bit more notice, but I knew it must've been a hassle for her to mentally accept the invitation to begin with, considering her history.

"What time are we leaving?"

"Six a.m. tomorrow."

"All right." I mulled it over. "Give me until tonight to let you know?"

"Since it's a miracle you're even considering my offer, I'll let you have this." She giggled, skipped out happily, and I smiled after her.

After my brief meeting, I'd become focused on work when my phone went off. I glanced at it quickly but momentarily freaked out at the name. It was Marcus.

"*Lunch?*"

I looked at the time. It had flown by so fast I hadn't even noticed. But honestly, I didn't feel like meeting him. I didn't know why. Something about last night was nagging at me. No, not the kiss, but the restaurant. And how Cristo was the one to drag me out of there.

As great a guy as Marcus was, I couldn't help but feel like we'd started things too soon with that kiss. I felt like too much of a coward to really do anything about it. I was dreading him coming to my office if I said I couldn't make it.

If I thought about it, I really couldn't because I had to leave with Aubrey tomorrow. Yes! I had to wrap things up today by 6 p.m. and inform Lyra about my absence!

"Lyra!"

I found myself at the coffee shop anyway, my eye on the verge of twitching.

"I mean, you're leaving pretty suddenly," Marcus said with a tentative sip of his coffee.

"Yes, it was a last-minute thing." I nodded and bit into my sandwich a little too forcefully. "Aubrey just burst into my office about forty-five minutes ago and announced it."

"You know she can't force you to go, right?"

I blinked at him questioningly, a bit confused. Did I give off the impression I didn't want to go?

"I…she isn't?"

"I'm just saying." He began to sound defensive and waved his hand around. "Your job's pretty time consuming, so if you were to leave for a week, then—"

"I have a substitute." I was starting to sound defensive, too.

"What if she doesn't do as well as you?"

"It's just paperwork."

"Clients?"

"Three clients a month, and I've got my second one to attend to after South Korea."

"You just never know—"

"I think I know how to do my job pretty well, Marcus." I cut him off. "So what is this really about?"

There were alarms ringing in my head, but I couldn't quite put my finger on them just yet.

"I just…think we kind of left things hanging last night?" He shrugged.

"I said we should take it slow."

"How slow?"

"*Really* slow." I sounded almost robotic at this point. My body had become frozen in place, back straightened, and shoulders squared. My mouth was the only thing that was moving.

Silence stretched between us. Awkward, filled with invisible questions wrapping around me like a cage. They coiled around my throat warningly, ready to constrict me at any given moment.

I didn't need this right now.

"That…doesn't clear up much." He sighed, deflating in his seat as he reached for his coffee.

Silence again.

A minute…

Another minute…

"I don't know if…last night should've happened."

"Too soon?"

My tongue was like lead in my mouth.

"I'm not sure." I finally choked out. "Which is why I need to get away for a bit. Be with the girls. It's been a while since I've had this chance."

He nodded and straightened, pushing the slice of apple pie toward me.

"If that's how it is, then you should go."

Well, *now* I didn't want the pie.

Something irked me about the way he said it. Like he was giving me permission. But I knew I was overthinking this. I'd yet to recover from how abusive Mark was. I just needed to remind myself that Marcus wasn't the same guy. He just needed answers, that's all. He was only nervous about what happened and felt as lost as I did. Now that we'd communicated, it—

"I hope things won't be too awkward when you come back," he said. "I'd like to hang out like this more without *that* getting in the way."

"We can pretend it never happened...for now?"

He nodded. "Yeah."

"Cool."

"Okay."

"Hmm."

Silence once again.

"I should head back," I announced and rose to my feet. The untouched apple pie stared at me sadly.

I'll come back for you, lil' guy, I promise.

The park called me toward it once again. Talking with Marcus had taken a lot out of me for some reason. I still had time to kill and needed to recharge before I headed back.

Walking around, I searched in yearning for my spot by the pond.

The pond Cristo claimed was my *favorite*. I chuckled at the memory. I didn't know about it being my favorite, but it sure was peaceful there compared to the rest of the park since it was more toward the center rather than the outskirts.

I finally found it and led myself to the seat across from it, wobbling on the grass in my heels. Halfway there, I kicked them off in frustration and walked barefoot with a shoe in each hand. I could hear Cristo's laughter in my head as if he had been watching me.

"Ugh." I groaned as the nausea ran up my throat. Why was I thinking about him?

Sitting down, I stared at the pond blankly, wondering where the ducks had gone. I could hear their faint cries from somewhere in the distance, but that was it.

The breeze was soft, carrying with it the light chatter of people on the streets and the birds in the air. The sky was cloudy and looked grayer than before. Some of the trees were already turning orange. Fall was coming.

It was peaceful.

Maybe being alone is best for me, I decided internally. Yet, for some reason, I wasn't entirely convinced.

Chapter 11

I hadn't felt so excited for anything in my life. I couldn't sleep, and I felt a surge of relief flowing through me. No Mom, no Emily, no Marcus. And no Cristo.

I could finally catch a break.

Aubrey had sent me a list of essentials. Apparently, we'd be heading to a resort there with our very own open pool, which didn't make sense considering how cold it was starting to get. But I went with it and searched for any bikinis I had.

Hmm, I'll have to buy some, I realized while scanning my wardrobe. I hadn't visited the beach in ages.

I was surprised she was only taking three other people along. I thought Aubrey was the super-social kind. But then again, I didn't know much about her personal life outside her love life. My phone rang on top of a pile of clothes, and I noticed it was already 4:30 a.m. Aubrey wanted breakfast at the airport before we boarded the private jet, so we could all get acquainted with each other.

"*Do you want me to pick you up?*" read her message. "*We're all carpooling.*"

"*No, it's okay. I'll see you there!*" I sent back with a smiling emoji.

I finished packing the last of my items and reviewed my checklist one more time. Once I was satisfied with everything, I locked the case and swung my bag onto my shoulder, dialing Lyra to get the car.

It was a peaceful ride that seemed too short, but I could feel the stress flow out of me by the minute. Lyra chuckled next to me as she drove. "You're looking younger by the second."

"I feel younger, too." I chuckled back.

"I'm glad you're going." She sounded genuinely sincere. "You should do this more often."

"I'm surprised I didn't before." I sighed. "What was I thinking?"

"Not even on the bi-annual leave? Or even the holidays?"

"I'd still be working or doing workshops," I admitted. "For some reason, I thought I always needed to be busy. Not sure what I was running away from."

"Well," she said slowly and turned into a parking spot, "I hope you learn something from this getaway. It's nice seeing you like this."

I smiled at her and got out, eager to get out of this country.

It felt so surreal, stepping into the airport while it was still dark outside. I rolled the suitcase behind me and looked around for Aubrey. I could hear her squeal from the other side of the place and walked over quickly with my head down. I didn't bother taking off my sunglasses. I wasn't wearing any makeup and had opted for dark fitted jeans and a cashmere sweater. The others were dressed casually, too, which I was glad for.

Aubrey threw her arms around me. She looked so happy, and it made me feel even better to be here.

"So, you already know—"

"Alex!" I laughed. "I should've known."

She playfully rolled her eyes. "Kind of surprised you're surprised at all." I engulfed her in a hug but stepped back suspiciously as I sniffed her hair.

"Alex," I began warningly, "you're aware we're heading to South Korea."

"Yeah, what about it?" She chuckled.

"They have strict laws about marijuana."

"I don't think they'll sniff out pre-made edibles." She winked. I only shook my head.

"Also, I hope you remember Jenna Dupont?" Aubrey turned to a remarkably familiar pale, black-haired girl.

"Oh, I saw you at the Alexakis and Caron manor."

She blushed a little. "Ah, yes." Her accent was visibly French. "I was just there to…um, see a friend."

Oh, I reminded myself, *I'm not supposed to know she's Cristo's cousin.*

"I remember you from a restaurant, though," she said with a giggle. "A friend of mine paid the waiter to drop wine on your guest."

"Cristo really did that?" I stood there in shock. Alex and Aubrey exchanged confused looks while Jenna nodded in amusement.

"He was so concerned. I'm guessing you're a good friend of his."

"We're…acquaintances." I shrugged. Jenna didn't seem too satisfied by that answer, but she shook her head.

"Never mind, shall we all eat?"

The next fifteen hours on the jet were spent sleeping or reading, with the occasional bathroom break. Eating, too. For some reason, I was consuming a lot of their cream-filled éclairs. I only hoped I wasn't going to get my period two weeks earlier than I should because that would really suck. The others were starting to get bored out of their minds, too.

It was a blur when the jet landed, and we piled ourselves into a limo to be taken to the resort. Although the flight was as luxurious as it could be, I needed to stretch out my body. My muscles felt cramped and I needed a warm soak.

I was most grateful to find out that we all had separate suites in the same hallway. Without hesitating, I locked the door to the bathroom and kicked my clothes off. I was surprised to find it already filled with warm water. It smelled wonderful, peppered with flower petals and beads. Already feeling relieved, I lowered myself into the bathtub and sighed loudly.

It felt like all the stresses and strains of my life were being pulled out through my pores. I wasn't even afraid of falling asleep in it, and despite having slept on the plane, I could use a nice nap where I wasn't constrained to a semi-firm seat that hurt my back.

Just washing myself felt like such a chore, and I didn't feel like leaving the tub anytime soon. I knew I needed to head to bed and wake up in a few hours to wash my hair and get ready for the show. After ten minutes, I drained the tub and let the shower wash away any residue of essential oils and soap. Wrapping myself in a warm and fluffy bathrobe, I walked out and fell face-first onto the bed. Before I could even talk myself into getting up to unpack a pair of pajamas, I was out cold.

I woke up to my phone ringing in my bag beside me. Sitting up groggily, I reached over to search for it.

"Hello?"

"Are you up? We're going to leave in an hour and a half for the show?"

"I'm up now," I said with a good stretch. "And hungry, too. Are we going to eat?"

"We're heading to the dining room in ten minutes."

"All right, I'll see you there."

Working through the lead-like feeling in my body, I pushed myself out of bed and got dressed. Heading down to the dining hall, I saw mostly Koreans who likely lived abroad as compared to foreign visitors. It felt nice. We got comfortable and ordered a mix of their traditional dishes with more familiar cuisine.

I realized how different it was being here with Aubrey, Jenna, and Alex. I hadn't had a girls' day out in forever. Or at all, really. I always just tended to avoid everyone because of the preconceived notions of being hurt, but right now, I felt so much more comfortable than I ever had before. Dare I say it, even better than being around Marcus.

Why hadn't I done this sooner?

I didn't even notice the time flying by as we laughed and talked about anything and everything *but* men. Aubrey had started talking to people she'd worked with in the past. She was trying hard to get back into the fashion scene. Jenna was a phenomenal poet and writer who had made her debut a few months earlier. Alex was called up by a food show producer for weed-infused recipes, which sounded like a lot of fun.

"What about you?" Jenna asked me. "Anything exciting?"

"Honestly," I chuckled, "this trip is the most exciting thing that's happened to me in my whole life. I just finally decided I was tired of working as a distraction and worrying about money when I didn't need to anymore."

"I mean, you're the best matchmaker in New York," Aubrey affirmed. "It's a surprise you don't take more time off for yourself."

"You're also very strategic, I've heard," Jenna said. "I heard you hold a good portion of shares in some companies."

"I plan ahead." I shrugged nonchalantly and sipped my green tea to avoid any more questions. "By the way, how much time do we have before leaving?"

Alex checked her watch. "We should really get going right now if we're gonna make it on time, to be honest."

Chapter 12

The glitz and glamor of it all, as beautiful and mesmerizing as it was, gave me a headache. Too many photographers, music too loud and it was too cold. It smelled like paint and smoke. Artificial. The jewelry glinted into my eyes, and the whispers tickled my ears and made it unbearable to even be there.

I'd made a mistake. Fashion shows were absolutely not for me.

I felt Jenna's hand on mine, gentle and concerned. I looked at her and she nodded in understanding, turning to whisper to Aubrey and taking me away to the bathroom. I followed her without hesitation and looked in the mirror, a little shocked. My neck and cheeks were flushed, making my freckles pop.

"Are you feeling okay?"

"I don't know." I laughed and shook my head. "Guess I'm not a fan of crowded spaces."

"It was noisy, too," she agreed with a solemn nod. I splashed some cold water on my face, hoping my mascara wouldn't run down even though it was waterproof. I'd kept makeup on me anyway but didn't want to take the time to fix it because I felt so drained.

I breathed deeply as I patted my face dry with a towel. Jenna stared down at her shoes as she leaned back against the wall. She seemed expectant, as if she were grasping at the right words to say.

"You know," she began, "I heard you're very convincing as a matchmaker. You talk to parents well."

"I've heard that, too, but I can't speak for myself."

"What if I wanted to hire you?"

I looked at her and she seemed nervous. Extremely nervous. I turned around and rested my hip against the edge of the sink, crossing my arms. "Well, I don't come cheap, obviously."

"I don't mind." She chuckled. "I just need someone reputable to at least try something for me. I can't tell you yet, but I've heard you're good at special requests."

"If it was Aubrey that told you anything—"

"Austin Santiago."

I froze as my mind flashed back to the men I saw sitting in the bar, the day Aubrey told me about her suspicions of Fernando cheating on her.

"Oh…" I trailed off, sitting on the sink and gripping the edge tightly. "I'll admit, that case was a bit of a nightmare. You're lucky we're in a more tolerant time. But I can't guarantee anything, you know? Each clients' circumstances are different."

"I'm biding my time," she said in an understanding tone. "I'll call you when I'm more financially independent from my family."

"I'll do what I can."

It wasn't long before we found ourselves outside. We walked around carefree, and I was already feeling much better. It wasn't any less crowded outside but there was space to move. Jenna and I got along great, and I felt young again. I wished I'd tried making more friends when I was younger, although there was only a four-year difference between us.

I was a little tipsy, feeling the laughter bubble up in my throat with the obscure jokes and observations we were throwing at each other. Things started to speed up and it all happened so fast. In a single second, Jenna had disappeared. I could still feel the warmth of her hand on my bicep, but she was nowhere to be seen. I could hear her somewhere in the wind, but the crowd pulled me away. I thought it would be better to follow her voice and cross the road to wait on the pavement until the traffic cleared up and I could look for her.

When the light turned green, cars sped onto the road and I couldn't see to the other side where I hoped Jenna would be standing. When the light turned red, she wasn't there.

I reached into my purse and panicked at the low battery. My phone could die any second now.

Just my luck, I groaned internally and tossed it back inside. *I need to find her.*

My feet carried me wherever they could, retracing our steps onto all the streets and the stores. As the night grew darker, the crowd started to thin out, leaving only small groups and individual people rushing to get home.

I needed to return to the hotel, but not without Jenna and the girls.

Turning helplessly into a dimly lit alleyway, I froze.

How did I get here?

My breath came out in small puffs of white, and beads of sweat formed on my forehead as I realized I didn't recognize where I was at all. I'd been roaming around mindlessly the entire time, and now I was lost.

Clanging. Metal against metal. Repeated, slow, and…almost mocking.

Someone laughed in the darkness. Wait, not one, but a few. There were more. Deep voices aimed right at me.

I was standing under a single lightbulb. My heart was thudding so loud in my chest that it felt as if they could hear it. I needed it to calm down.

"Hey, you…" a guy slurred in a thick accent as he stumbled out of the darkness toward me. "You're lost, ha? We help."

I remained quiet and slowly moved back toward the darkness. I knew if I ran around the corner, I'd find a shop to hide inside.

"It is okay," another slurred.

No, it's not, I thought in alarm as another man came out of the darkness. Now there were three of them. I needed to run.

Without a second thought, I turned around and sprinted. Their laughter followed me, as if they'd lassoed their voices onto my ankles. I could hear them stumbling and running behind me trying to catch up in their drunken haze. I just knew they could hear the blood rushing in my ears like I could. They were following it.

My heart was in my throat. I would either die tonight, or worse…

"Lilith!" I heard someone call out in the distance. Another man but…familiar.

Oh, my God…

"Lilith!"

"I'm here!"

His hurried footsteps on the asphalt sounded closer to me than the ones behind me, and he came into view. The neon sign of the shop next to him fell onto his figure like a halo that called out to me. "Lilith!"

He opened his arms as my legs pumped harder trying to outrun the shadows. I fell into him just centimeters out of the alley's ominous darkness that would've swallowed me whole. The harsh cold of the wind was replaced with a warmth so comforting, I could've melted.

"Jenna was so worried," he said in a rushed panic and grabbed me by the shoulders to look at me. My breath caught in my lungs as he examined me with his eyes holding a literal storm in them. "Are you okay? What were you running from?"

"Yah!" the drunken men yelled from behind me, and Cristo pulled me away to shield me behind himself.

"*Mwol balae?*" he snapped at them. I had no idea what that meant.

The men laughed, saying something mockingly in Korean, to which Cristo snapped back. Whatever he said must've been serious because the guys backed off.

"Come on," he said, voice doing a one-eighty and becoming absolutely gentle.

I was stunned...

We headed to the main road where he'd parked an obviously rented car. There were other cars honking impatiently and he yelled at them apologetically while opening the passenger door for me. I slid inside shakily. He soon entered the driver's side and drove off immediately.

The ride was silent. All the way to the resort. I couldn't speak as we entered the elevator. My legs were trembling like jelly and I did my best to hold myself up. As soon as we reached our floor, I mindlessly walked off toward my suite. He followed inconspicuously. I could tell he was trying to respect my space and keep a comfortable distance.

I unlocked the door and walked in, holding it open. He studied me carefully as I kept my head down, but walked in. He found the couch across the bed and sat down awkwardly. I closed the door and locked it, heading toward my bed to sit down.

"What are you doing here?" My voice was softer than I meant it to be as I wrung my fingers. I hated it. It didn't sound strong, or confident, or annoyed. Just…broken and tired.

"An international architecture expo that I'm a part of," he explained. "Jenna called as soon as you disappeared. Your phone was dead."

"Yeah," I whispered.

"Lilith," he began gently and leaned forward, "did they do anything? Did they touch you?"

I shook my head, not trusting myself to speak over the bile rising in my throat, as I prepared for him to berate me about being out so late on my own and getting lost as if it was my fault. And truth be told, it was.

"I'm sorry you had to go through that." His voice became even softer. "I…I can't imagine how scared you must've been."

I was having flashback memories. So many memories. Especially of the night I had to interview Cristo six years ago. And I realized, that so far, he was the only man I knew who had protected me. But I was waiting for the blade to drop and cut through the sense of security my mind tried to feel when I was around him. The tears sprang into my eyes, and I bit my lip hard to hold them at bay.

"I'm sorry for worrying you guys," I whispered.

"Of course we'd be worried," he explained. "We care about you"

"I should've been more careful."

He sighed and got up, pulling the vanity stool over to sit closer to me.

"Lilith, you can't *ever* be careful enough."

"It could've been avoided if—"

"Nooo, listen to me." His voice grew stern and he pulled my hands gently into his. "I don't know exactly what to say in this situation because I'm not a woman, but all I know is that when a piece of shit wants to hurt you, *nothing* you do will stop him. It's not up to you to take responsibility for their bullshit."

I broke down, sobbing and shaking uncontrollably. It was too much. I felt too much. There was so much pain in my chest, weighing on my heart like a rock.

He held onto my hands tighter and softly reassured me, "It wasn't your fault."

The rock lifted, and hot, intense tears of rage and humiliation that I'd forgotten I had, began pooling out of my eyes, nose, and mouth. I was ugly crying, short of breath, and at my absolute weakest. Cristo reached out for the box of tissues on the bedside table and handed them to me.

"Can I stay with you, please?" His voice was almost a whisper. "Do you need me to hold you?"

I nodded. I needed the warmth I felt just like when he'd found me. I needed it so much that I couldn't make sense of anything else. He didn't hesitate to come over and sit next to me and brought me into his arms. I buried myself into his chest as he held onto me securely. It wasn't a half-assed hug, but a real one. He wasn't holding back; he knew I needed comfort.

I'd probably ruined his shirt, but his hand rubbing my back and shoulders showed he didn't mind. He kept asking small questions, like if I needed water, or if I wanted him to turn the heater on, or should he run me a warm bath. I would nod and shake my head in response, only focused on how his presence engulfed me and made me forget how unsafe I'd felt just a little while ago.

It was a while until I started to quiet down, slowly slipping from soft sobs to little sniffles. I had calmed down considerably when he reached over for the bottle on the bedside table and opened it for me, never letting go of me completely.

"You need to wash up and change into something comfortable." His voice was low as he handed me the bottle. "Do you need me to stay until you're asleep?"

I nodded, still feeling too weak to speak. He helped me stand up, saying something about unpacking my suitcase for me. I wordlessly went to the bathroom to take care of myself. Ten minutes later, I saw my comfy silk pajamas laid out for me. The same ones reserved for a good cry.

"I gotta use the bathroom for a bit. You should change."

"There are extra toothbrushes in the cabinet if you need one."

He locked the bathroom and I changed into my pajamas quickly, getting into the warm bed and under the covers. It was soft, and I cocooned myself into it snugly and quickly drifted off to sleep.

Chapter 13

I woke up in the middle of the night, a little confused and somewhat panicked. I wasn't sure why, I knew I'd just had a nightmare, but I couldn't remember any of the details. The lights in the room were off, but there was a dim light from the outside spilling in under the door.

It outlined Cristo's silhouette. He sat on the stool, arms crossed on the bed, leaning forward and his head resting on them as he snored away softly. I felt so bad for him.

Tentatively, I reached out for him, unsure if what I was doing was appropriate. I just wanted him to sleep okay and not be too tired to drive back home.

"Cristo," I whispered with a gentle hand on his shoulder. I nudged him just enough for him to open his eyes. He blinked sleepily and lifted his head, yawning wide.

"Hi." He grunted tiredly, and oh, my *fucking* goodness—what was his voice doing to me?

I felt so embarrassed at the very sensual reaction my body had to it that I pulled the comforter over my chest. Not that he would be able to see anything in the dark, but the blush on my cheeks wasn't discreet in the fact that I felt kind of…turned on.

"You shouldn't sleep like that," I murmured. "You can sleep next to me."

He seemed way too tired to protest and he immediately climbed up, staying on the comforter so there was an appropriate barrier between us. He sighed as if content, placing and arm over his eyes to fall back to sleep. He was undeniably attractive when he was asleep.

I looked at him curiously, wondering how he managed to just…be himself. So carefree and happy. Had he never suffered any hardship at all? I felt a little jealous at how easily he could fall back asleep.

He opened an eye to look at me and I gasped, tearing my gaze away from him.

"Can't sleep?"

"I don't know," I quickly said, soft and confused.

He was silent for a moment. I felt him shuffle a bit and looked at him out of the corner of my eye. He turned on his side toward me.

"If you're still…I dunno, shaken? I'm right here."

"This is the third time you've saved me," I said suspiciously. "How do you always end up at the right place just when I need somebody?"

He breathed deeply and glanced behind me. "I've been asking myself the same thing, really. But I promise I'm not stalking you."

I stared down at my hand on the comforter and sighed, tracing random invisible doodles onto the fabric.

"I hate believing in fate and all," I started softly. "Everything I did was on my own and for myself, you know?"

"Mrs. Beaumont mentioned that about you," he replied almost too carefully. "Hyper-independence."

"So that means I don't believe in luck, either."

"Is that why you blame yourself when things go wrong?"

I froze and kept my eyes down.

"Lilith," he whispered. It sounded so intimate. I couldn't help but look at him. I tried hard to breathe but goodness, he looked absolutely heavenly as the light caught his warm skin and silver eyes. "What if fate did exist, just for a moment? What would you do?"

I didn't know what it was about the way he said it, but things just clicked in place. I found his gaze holding me steady. No words were exchanged as the energy in the air sparked onto my skin and kick-started my heart into a new rhythm. The ripple spread through my chest, and I could feel my skin literally wake up to him. His eyes, curious and warm, felt like they were beckoning me over. And I just…couldn't refuse.

Slowly raising myself to crawl over to him, he wasted no time in propping himself onto his elbow and reaching out for me halfway, his hand landing on mine as I neared him. His fingers slid delicately up my wrist, carefully holding my elbow as our faces halted mere millimeters from each other, noses touching and breaths mixing. I could practically feel his lips brush ever so lightly against mine and…

I gave in and kissed him, almost moaning into his mouth from the way my heart exploded in my chest. A small gasp escaped my mouth and his breath hitched ever so slightly at that. His kiss was so soft and gentle; it stole my breath. The dizziness was more exhilarating than uncomfortable, and his hand sliding to the back of my head made it so much better for me to even consider moving closer lest he take it away.

He shifted to sit up and I broke out of my trance, crawling over to him all the way and letting him guide me onto his lap. He was visibly flustered and looking at his long lashes flutter as his shy eyes studied my face made me feel kind of flattered. Although, I was aware I didn't look any less breathless. His chest rose and fell against mine slowly, and he gulped. I should've felt embarrassed, knowing he could feel my nipples perked up against him, but I wasn't.

I really wanted him.

His hand cupped my cheek and drew me in. Our mouths met gently but moved with so much passion that I was quite literally melting between my thighs. I whimpered a little as I felt a hard rod prodding against my pajama bottoms. He groaned and grabbed my waist, running his hand up and down my back as if he were restraining himself from ravishing me completely. My sensitive skin made my back arch, pressing my chest into him. We were getting desperate by the minute, as he parted his lips slightly to swipe my lip with his tongue. I let him in and groaned loudly at how amazing his tongue felt against mine.

"Fuck, Lilith," he grunted as his hands fell to my hips with a firm grip. "I…dammit."

"I don't mind," I whispered into his mouth. As soon as I said that he practically melted against me, leaning forward to kiss me harder as he pulled me backward onto the bed. Keeping his hands on my thighs, he propped them around his waist and rolled his hips into mine instinctively.

"Oh…" My mouth fell open in a gasp. "Mmh."

"Was that—"

"It's fine." I cut him off and pulled him down to kiss me. I felt his shaft pressing against his pants and lined against my clit so deliciously that I didn't want him to stop rocking himself against me. My hips bucked against him of their own accord, making him moan lightly in my mouth. My breasts were swollen with arousal, and I wanted so much for him to touch my body wherever he pleased.

It seemed like he was reading my mind as his hands slipped under my shirt, travelling up my warm, bare skin. I only noticed that he had been discreetly undoing the buttons when my top suddenly fell away, and I felt the air on my chest. His lips moved down my jaw to my neck, where he sucked and licked lightly. I was losing my breath as his hand inched toward my breast, finally cupping it under his large, warm hand and brushing a delicate thumb over my nipple.

The air left my body.

"Did you like that?" he murmured against my skin. I could only nod. What followed was the most pleasurable feeling of his warm and damp tongue circling my nipple, making me moan out. His hands stayed firmly on my hips as he rubbed his hard-on against my hot and wet sex.

He needed to get rid of his clothes *right now*. I'd never, *ever* wanted someone as much as I wanted him in that moment.

With a mind of their own, my hands urgently shot out to the hem of his pants, untucking his shirt, and unbuttoning them. His hands clamped around my wrists. I looked at him nervously as he pinned my arms over my head and pressed his mouth gently to mine. I sighed, and barely registered him crossing my wrists to hold them with one hand. I relished his kiss, eyes closed as his hands moved away. Instinctively, I reached out for his neck, fingers wandering around aimlessly to his now bare, warm chest.

God, he was toned. His tongue caressed mine as I let my hands splay against him, travelling down his torso. He groaned a little in my mouth as his cock pressed urgently against my very wet sex. My hips bucked against his, moving slowly as my fingers found the button of his pants.

He was touching me everywhere, lips travelling down my neck and making me whimper with anticipation. He lay himself down on top of me, our bare chests pressing tightly together, making me even more flustered than I already was and frustrated that his pants were still on. I felt his finger tug at my waistband. I lifted my hips, slipping them off quickly, waiting for him to give me what I wanted.

"*Oh, fuck!*" I gasped as his slick finger wiped up from my slick entrance to my clit, rubbing in delicate circles that drew out quick and desperate gasps. My face grew heated as he propped himself onto his elbow, staring down at my face with his eyes darker than a hurricane.

"You're absolutely gorgeous like this." His voice was so deep and guttural that it made my walls throb painfully. I looked away with an embarrassed moan. I could feel his gaze roaming over my skin and landing on my chest, seeing him licking his lips from the corner of my eye as he bent down to take a nipple into his mouth once more to suck on it gently.

I was about to lose my mind. His hand splayed out to cup my sex, massaging the lips in circles that sent my eyes rolling to the back of my head. And then came his finger, sliding in slowly inside me. It was hot, pulsating, and I squeezed my eyes together so tightly that it was bright white behind my lids. My vision grew faint again as he pumped it slowly inside of me, my back arching against his body with my mouth falling open in a silent scream. I gasped as he pushed in a second one out of nowhere, his pace growing quicker.

I felt his breath brush my lips as I moaned with each shot of pleasure that ran up my navel.

"Cristo," I breathed, "please…I need you to —*ah!*"

"Need me to what?" he whispered, and I swear I could hear the smirk in his voice.

"Just fuck me already."

"But I am."

I smacked him lightly across the arm and he laughed, kissing me roughly as he pulled his hand from between my legs, leaving me feeling cold and empty. I heard rustling as he moved around.

Grabbing my legs, he nestled himself between them and slapped my thighs lightly.

"You're really hot, you know?"

I groaned and covered my face in embarrassment, but my hands went flying to grab the sheets when I felt his warm, rock-hard shaft push against my entrance. I looked at his face, that smirky little shit, as he rubbed his bare cock against my sex and making me wetter than I could possibly be. But he finally showed mercy as he entered me in one swift motion, filling me up and making me scream.

"*Cristo*," I gasped loudly as he pounded into me in long hard strokes, "I—*oh, my fucking goodness!*"

"You like that?" he groaned.

But I couldn't speak anymore as my skin lit up, his hands on my hips blazing as his skin slapped against mine with each calculated thrust. I dug my fingers into the space between the mattress and headrest, trying to hold on as he then fucked me so hard and fast that my entire body bounced against the sheets.

"You're so pretty like this," he muttered, a hand sliding up to my ribs, stroking my skin gently before cupping my breast to brush his thumb over my nipple. I groaned loudly as he leaned forward slightly so that he was now pressing against my clit as we moved against each other.

I don't know how long we were at it, riding each other like there was no tomorrow. But it was tomorrow, because the sun came up and I was still beneath him, desperate for his touch, his warmth, and all of his attention.

I'd never orgasmed so hard in my life.

Chapter 14

My bed was too warm when I woke up, and so was I. Slowly regaining consciousness, I blinked the sleep away.

The memories rushed in and I froze in place, realizing that I wasn't alone. My back was pressed against Cristo's strong chest, his hand draped over my stomach. His breath brushed over my collarbone and I realized his head was in my neck, lips pressed unconsciously to my jaw.

I was going to be turned on and ready for round two if I didn't get out of his hold quickly. My face flushed as I remembered the way he flipped me onto my side to fuck me from behind, grabbing my waist to hold me in place and caressing my breasts. He'd made me orgasm so violently that I fell asleep as soon as I came down from my high.

How loud was I last night?

Cristo grunted softly in my ear as he shuffled a bit. I closed my eyes immediately and pretended to sleep, deepening my breath to make sure he couldn't tell.

His head lifted off my skin, his hand moving to rest on my hip for a moment. He didn't move, except for his thumb that brushed my skin slowly. It was unsure. With a sigh, he moved away from me carefully. I laid still and listened to him move around. The door shut softly.

He was gone. Just like that.

I was left in a daze trying to process if it had all really happened.

I sat with the girls at the table, blankly staring at the view outside as we were served breakfast. The three of them talked, but I knew there was a strain in the air. They probably knew.

Jenna touched my shoulder gently and I turned to her. She gave me a concerned look.

"You want to get away for a bit after breakfast?"

I only nodded, looked at the omelet before me and decided to dig in. Twenty minutes later, I found myself by the pool with Jenna. She'd changed into a white one-piece and sat beside me with her feet in the pool. I stuck to shorts and a sports bra, my hair thrown into a bun.

"How are you feeling right now?"

"I'm not sure." I sighed. "Mostly empty and confused."

Silence.

"I, um…" I began, "I came here to get away from all the drama back home. Away from Marcus and Cristo. I just needed some me time with the girls, you know?"

She nodded in understanding, so I continued, "And I haven't dated in a very long time. I've never felt for anyone so deeply that makes me want to build on those connections. I don't know who I like and don't like."

"What's Marcus like?"

"Entertaining," I said with a small smile. "We can talk about anything and everything. We work hard and have coffee together. We're getting to know each other well."

"And…Cristo?"

Blank. I didn't know him as much as I would've liked to before everything that happened last night. But I was the one who initiated it so…I couldn't really complain.

"I don't know him very well." I sighed. "I don't know him the way I know Marcus. He and I have barely talked. We're not even really friends, we just keep randomly bumping into each other ever since the Alexakis and Caron's party."

She nodded. "I think Cristo cares for you a lot."

"I'm not sure I feel the same for him," I sighed, "nor would I want to."

"Why not?"

"I don't know." I shook my head. "I just… Marcus doesn't ask me to let my guard down, you know? But Cristo makes me want to when I don't even know what he'll do next."

Jenna gave me a confused look, and rightfully so. I was confused, too.

"I just can't let anyone in like that." I tried to explain. "Not right now at least. I don't feel ready for any kind of like…commitment or even a casual arrangement. Whatever happened last night was on a whim and I shouldn't have allowed it."

But you liked it, a part of me whispered. I pushed it away. As much as I wanted to acknowledge, that for the first time ever, I'd really enjoyed sex…I just couldn't bring myself to do it.

I needed to stay away from Cristo. As far as I could.

"Would you like me to ask him to keep his distance?"

"Yes, thank you."

Coward, said my conscience. Yes, I was a coward. I didn't want to confront him, or talk to him, or see him, or even be around him with a blindfold on.

My phone vibrated, and I saw Marcus's face pop up on the screen. I felt so annoyed that I wanted to throw my phone into the water. Jenna must've seen the expression on my face because she reached down and locked my screen.

"You're busy right now," she said nonchalantly. "He'll understand. Come on, let's swim."

I gave her a grateful look and she smiled back, slipping into the water and reaching out to pull me in. I let her and we splashed around for a while until Aubrey and Alex joined us. And soon enough, I'd forgotten about everything that had happened before.

We spent the rest of the week visiting cute restaurants, popular tourist spots, and shopping for clothes. When it was time to go back, I almost felt sad that it had to end.

And then I remembered Marcus had said he'd wait for me at the airport. I groaned immediately when we landed, hoping he wasn't being serious. As much as I wanted to hang out with him, I still wanted to relish the time away from him.

"It's not like you told him when we were landing, right?" Jenna whispered to me as we walked through the terminal. "I mean, I'm sure he wouldn't be determined enough to wait a few hours just to make sure he'd catch you."

"The guy gives me stalker vibes," Alex announced in a matter-of-fact tone. Aubrey smacked her arm. "But it's *true*. I can tell!"

"You can't just assume stuff like that about people," Aubrey huffed. "Besides, he's a fairly attractive and rich doctor, I don't think he needs to chase after anyone."

"If we see him, can we run the other way and you guys just drop me home?"

"Too late." Jenna sighed. I turned my head and saw Marcus standing in the waiting area, waving over at me. In that moment, I kind of hated him. I wished he could read between the lines and pick up on cues.

"Maybe you need to be more open with him about your boundaries," Jenna suggested, "because men are a little slow."

"He's kinda like a golden retriever." Aubrey stroked her chin.

Alex scoffed. "More like a psychotic Chihuahua."

Jenna laughed while I rolled my eyes at the two of them bickering with each other. Marcus approached us slowly, and I broke away from the girls to walk toward him. He opened his arms, which I wasn't expecting. I gave him an awkward hug, pulling away quickly.

"You didn't have to come."

"Of course I did." He chuckled. "I can't imagine how tired you must be from a flight that long."

"It was all right."

He took my suitcase, and I waved the girls away. Alex gave us suspicious looks and signaled me to call her when I got home. I smiled at her in assurance and walked away with Marcus out of the airport and into his car.

I closed my eyes and rested my head on the headrest, hoping he wouldn't want to make small talk as he drove. He turned the radio on and lowered the volume, the deep bass of rap music reverberating around the car. That was annoying.

He was kind of annoying. This was weird. We were fine when I left last week. Was it because of the kiss? Was that why he was doing all this? Perhaps he still expected something to happen.

"How was your trip?"

"It was nice."

The music filled the silence, but it lay heavily on us.

"Anything eventful happen?"

I turned my head away as heat crept up my neck, memories from the wild night with Cristo resurfacing. I realized with horror that I needed to go to Barry Hall's wedding in two days. He would be there, and I wasn't sure if I was ready to face him on my own yet.

"Speaking of eventful," I muttered, unable to believe what I was about to do. I looked at him, perhaps a little too desperately. "Do you want to attend a friend's wedding as my plus one?"

End of Book 1

Printed in Great Britain
by Amazon